The Secret Lake

Karen Inglis

Cover illustration by Damir Kundalić

WS
Well Said Press
www.wellsaidpress.com

Published by Well Said Press 2011
83 Castelnau, London, SW13 9RT, England

ISBN : 978-0-9569323-0-3

This edition uses UK English.

www.wellsaidpress.com

This story is dedicated to my mother and father – and to all children who love to dream

Acknowledgements

With thanks to The Writers' Advice Centre for Children's books for advising me on how to reshape the plot in its early days. Also to my good friend Bridget Rendell for suggesting further useful revisions.

Thank you to my cover illustrator, Damir Kundalic, and to Rachel Lawston for helping us finalise the updated cover design in 2018.

Finally, thank you to Jessica and Tom whose magical communal gardens in West London inspired this story.

Come and play in the garden of imagination
Let the seeds of your dreams
Grow and blossom
In distant lands and times forgotten

London 2011

1 - The Gardener

Tom's face felt so hot he was sure it was about to explode. The midday sun beat down mercilessly on his back, and the beads of sweat that had long since formed on his forehead began to itch and tickle. But still he dug on. Surely if he kept going there would be a sign. A tuft of silky fur perhaps? A distant squeak? Or (and this really would be the best!) a pair of tiny eyes squinting blindly up towards the daylight.

He paused to wipe the trickling sweat with the back of his wrist, then lifted his spade for what felt like the one hundredth time - just as a dark shadow loomed up from behind. A familiar chill travelled down his spine as, with heart pounding, he swivelled round to meet the piercing stare of the gardener, Charlie Green.

'Now look 'ere, Tom Hawken, I've told you before, I've enough trouble chasing up these darn molehills without 'avin' you goin' round diggin' 'em up.'

Tom felt his cheeks burning which was odd because his body was suddenly freezing. Charlie Green had had it in for him since the day they had moved to the gardens, of that he was sure. He was always giving him funny looks.

Tom tried to speak, but his throat, which suddenly felt drier than the Sahara at noon, stuck tight. He never had been brilliant at getting out of trouble - just expert at getting into it.

Charlie Green squinted darkly. 'Next time, I'll 'ave to tell yer mum!' he growled. 'Now, take that rag o' yours and be off.'

Tom fumbled as he gathered up the corners of his Treasure Rag. To his relief, Charlie Green hadn't noticed the array of plant bulbs he had dug up, which now lay scattered in amongst his 'earth treasure' - three handsome stones, a piece of broken green bottle and a tatty old purse that had probably belonged to a child's doll. The stones he would keep and place in his box marked 'Tom's Earth Treasure', which sat in the grate of his enormous bedroom fireplace. Everything else he would throw back.

By the time he nudged open the small gate separating his parents' small patio garden from the main communal gardens Charlie Green had already re-filled the mole hole and was now stomping angrily across the lawns towards his shed. Clusters of tiny earth mounds lay scattered all around; it had been a bad week for moles in West London.

~

Tom's heart still took off every time he entered his first floor bedroom: after his tiny room in their tenth floor Hong Kong apartment it really was a dream come true! His ceiling reached high, like a private indoor sky; the narrow French doors, opening onto the tiny sun-filled balcony, stood tall as skyscrapers, and on the far wall a magnificent marble fireplace stood even taller than he was. But, more important than all of these things, was the view. Tom's new room looked out onto a vast rambling garden that stretched as far as the eye could see. The garden, which was shared by all of the houses in the square, was filled with clusters of rhododendron bushes and sprawling oak trees whose branches seemed to brush the passing clouds.

Tom pressed his nose hard against the French door window and breathed in deeply, still wondering about Charlie Green. Then, through his clouds of warm breath on the glass, he saw a small dog shoot out from a cluster of trees and race across the lawn towards the houses. Slowly, Tom's mouth widened into a grin. 'I DON'T BELIEVE IT, STELL!' he yelled at the top of his voice. 'HARRY'S BACK!'

Stella, who was lying on her bed in her room next door studying her friendship bracelet, didn't answer. With her iPhone music on full volume, she was busy hoping that her friends back in Hong Kong, who would all be asleep now, had thought about her today. She also

3

happened to be crunching her fifth fruit polo of the day – lime-green flavour to be precise - the one that always made her ears tingle. 'Tom thinks he's in heaven,' she had just messaged her best friend, Hannah, on Facebook. 'But it's so deathly dull here – all molehills and boys!'

Stella didn't budge. Nor, for that matter, did Tom who was now leaning out so far over his balcony he was in danger of falling off. He was determined to see if old Mrs Moon would be at her gate to welcome her disappearing dog. Of course she wasn't. After all, she would have to be psychic to know exactly *when* Harry would choose to come home. Never mind psychic, all the garden residents thought Mrs Moon was batty. Her 'Lost Dog' notices were pinned up everywhere and she drove them all mad phoning them up each time Harry went off, which was often for days at a time.

Tom had found himself wondering about Harry when he was out digging. The little long-haired terrier's comings and goings seemed to be part of garden life - as did the snarling Charlie Green and the molehills and, of course, the dotty old Mrs Moon. But why did the dog keep disappearing? And exactly where did he go? As thoughts of Charlie Green quickly evaporated, Tom resolved to solve Harry's mystery by summer's end.

2 - Beneath the Mound

'I wonder where Harry's gone this time,' Stella murmured as the sound of their mother's piano playing wafted through the morning breeze. Harry had been missing for almost a week and Mrs Moon was beside herself. (As a result, so were most of the garden residents.)

Tom and Stella were sitting on their favourite mound of grass on 'The Island'. The Island was a cluster of four oak trees in the centre of the garden skirted by rhododendron bushes. Stella twirled her friendship bracelet – a present from Hannah when they had left Hong Kong. 'Neither time nor distance will break our bond,' Hannah had said dramatically when she'd given it to her. How much those words meant now!

'I wonder where Harry goes *every* time,' Tom said with a frown as he picked at the mound of grass with his trowel.

'Don't do that!' snapped Stella. 'If Charlie Green catches you, you'll be–'

'*HEY! What's this?*' Tom's eyes locked open as he sat

5

staring between his legs at the ground.

'What's *what?*' Stella leaned forward as Tom continued scraping grass off the top of the mound beneath him.

'I think it's real treasure!' he shrieked. Sure enough, as Tom carried on digging, and his eyes continued to widen, underneath they could see what looked like the rounded lid of a wooden container - a real treasure chest.

Suddenly Stella clutched Tom's arm.

'Ouch! Let go, will you!' he squealed.

'*Shh..!*' hissed Stella, sitting bolt up and staring straight ahead. The bushes opposite rustled. Stella and Tom sat still as statues. If Charlie Green appeared now they were done for.

'Must have been a bird,' whispered Tom, finally letting out a breath. The bush was still again. He looked down and carried on digging. 'It's a box, and it's got grooves on the lid!' he gasped. The rounded lid of the treasure chest seemed to go on forever as the patch Tom dug grew wider and wider.

And then Stella's pale blue eyes widened.

'Tom!' she whispered in disbelief. 'It's not a box! It's a *boat!*'

'A boat?' said Tom. 'It can't be a boat, stupid, there's no water around here!'

At that moment the bush opposite trembled violently. They really had had it this time; they knew Charlie Green's breathless snort anywhere. He was probably crawling through the undergrowth to take them by surprise.

Then, with a final sharp rustle, the leaves ahead parted and out into the clearing appeared... Harry.

'Harry!' they cried.

'He's *soaking*!' exclaimed Stella.

Harry took one look at Tom and Stella, then turned towards home and fled.

'Wait, Harry!' Tom began to take chase. But it was too late. Harry streaked like lightning out past the rhododendron bushes and across the sun-drenched lawn. Mrs Moon didn't know it yet, but she was in for a very pleasant surprise.

~

'Tom, *come back!*'

Tom gave up his chase about half way across the lawn, just as their mother's voice echoed across the garden. 'Tom, Stella! Come on! We're leaving!'

'Help me with this.' Stella was dragging a log across the lawn towards the mound. 'If Charlie Green finds this mess we'll be grounded indoors for a week!'

Tom looked despondent. He had just unearthed the greatest treasure of his digging career and here he was being told he had to cover it up again.

'But I want to get the boat out!' he protested.

'We haven't got time! We're going to grandma's!' said Stella breathlessly. 'Quick, take that end.' They shuffled three or four steps sideways and lowered the log down on top of the mound.

Tom stepped back and kicked the log in frustration.

'Look,' said Stella firmly, 'it's no use making a fuss now. We'll come back tomorrow and see if we can find out where Harry came from.'

Tom's face twisted into a puzzled frown. 'What do you mean by that?'

'Well,' said Stella, tearing at the wrapping of her sweet packet, 'where there's a boat there must be water.' She popped an orange polo into her mouth and raised her eyebrows in excitement. '*I* think Harry knows where that water is - and it's *somewhere around here!*'

3 - Dawn Escape

Funnily enough it was Stella who had trouble sleeping that night. Tom, in his room next door, was out like a light the moment his head touched the pillow.

'A boat!' Stella whispered repeatedly. 'How on earth could it have got there? And why was Harry soaked to the skin?' She was thinking how first thing tomorrow they would have a good scout around in the bushes when a hollow clank from somewhere outside made her sit up. The clock at her bedside read 5 a.m. She must have fallen asleep. Still thinking about Harry she crept from her bed to her window. The sun hadn't risen and the garden was bathed in a grey early morning mist. Nothing. It must have been a dream. But then, as she was about to drop back the curtains, the clanking echoed again. Stella peered to the right, in the direction it seemed to have come from. A high-pitched squeak, followed by another clank. Then, through the dim half-light she spotted Harry - trotting across the lawn in the direction of The Island. The clanking must have been him trying to nudge open Mrs Moon's patio garden gate.

'Tom, quick! Wake up!' Stella tugged violently at Tom's pyjamas.

'What? Where's the mole? *Get it off me!*'

'Oh, wake up will you!' Stella snapped in a whisper. Tom sat up in a damp sweat. He had been dreaming that a friendly mole had just started to attack him.

'What's going on?' he mumbled, as his sister's face loomed in front of him in the dark.

'It's Harry! He's gone off again - I've just seen him!'

Tom immediately woke right up then fell on the floor as he tried to jump out of bed in a hurry. 'Let's get after him!' he squealed, diving for his dressing gown. Moments later, they stood at the top of the hallway stairs.

'Quietly!' mouthed Stella, glaring like a schoolteacher. Slowly they crept down, then put on their trainers and slipped outside into the grey morning air. 'Come on, we haven't got much time!' Stella whispered. She grabbed Tom's hand and together they raced across the damp grass towards The Island wearing only their pyjamas, dressing gowns and trainers.

'Drat! We've missed him!' said Stella. They had hunted around The Island for a good five minutes. All was still and there was no sign of Harry. But at least the log was still in place, which meant Charlie Green hadn't noticed their digging. 'We'll just have to come back and have a good look when it's light,' she said with a sigh. They then squelched back across the lawn, their trainers soaked with early morning dew.

It was about half way back that something caught the corner of Tom's eye. He glanced to his right and, through the fading dawn mist, for a moment thought he saw a group of three or four moles scampering in a circle on the grass. But when he blinked they had gone. The half-light was playing tricks on him. Cold and shivering they returned to their beds and slept soundly.

~

The ring of the telephone shattered the early morning calm.

'Hello… Oh, no, Mrs Moon, not again. I *am* sorry. Yes, of course we'll let you know if we see him. Of course. We'll call you right away. Goodbye, Mrs Moon.'

As they lay in their separate bedrooms, Tom and Stella listened to their mother's conversation, each thinking how their earlier jaunt really hadn't been a dream after all, and how, after breakfast, they must continue their search for Harry.

4 - The Secret Lake

By 10 o'clock Tom and Stella were back at the mound, complete with picnic lunch boxes. Stella, who was plugged into her iPhone music as usual, had brought a pocket torch for looking inside the bushes. For the first time in three weeks she also had a broad smile on her face. Tom had his red birthday binoculars slung round his neck, his digging trowel in one hand, and his treasure rag stuffed in his pocket.

'Right, we're going to have a good look inside this bush,' said Stella. She got down and crawled on all fours into the rhododendron bush that Harry had appeared from the morning before.

Tom quickly surveyed the garden with his binoculars, to see if Charlie Green was about. 'Coast clear! Coming in!' he shouted, but then immediately spotted something moving in the shade of one of the distant trees. Were those *moles* again? He refocused the binoculars to get a better look. But there was nothing there. 'I think I'm going bonkers!' he mumbled under his breath. Then he scrambled in after his sister yelling 'Ouch!' every few seconds as the binoculars thumped against his knees.

'Tom, be quiet!' snarled Stella after the fourth 'Ouch!' 'Do you want someone to hear us?' As they crawled deeper inside the thicket she switched on her tiny torch which shone a narrow beam of light ahead through the dark. Nothing. Only twigs, more twigs, green leaves, dead leaves, rotten flower heads and – ugh! - creepy crawlies scuttling back and forth across the undergrowth. The leaves brushing on Stella's hair suddenly gave her the shivers. 'There's nothing here, Tom,' she said, dusting imaginary beetles from the top of her head. 'Let's go back.'

Tom had just begun to manoeuvre himself round on the spot, twigs scratching at him from all sides, when his right arm slipped down a hole so deep that on one side he was suddenly up to his shoulder in undergrowth.

'Hey!' he bellowed, 'I've found a hole!'

Stella quickly crawled over and pulled him up, then pointed her torch to investigate. The hole was far wider than either of them could believe.

'Yikes, Tom, lucky you didn't fall right in!' she whispered. Stella shone the torch down into the darkness. 'Well, it's too big for a rabbit hole,' she said, flicking the beam of light up and down the inside wall.

'*Look!*' shrieked Tom, so suddenly that they both crashed backwards into the undergrowth. Stella sighed angrily, then leaned forward and held the beam of light still against the earth wall. To her astonishment, she could clearly see what Tom had spotted and she had nearly missed; a rusty metal ladder fixed against the earthen wall, and leading down into the hole.

'Shall we go down?' said Tom after they had both stared at the ladder for a minute. Stella didn't answer. Instead she took out a lime-green polo.

'Do you think the boat would fit down there?' she suddenly said. They both stared at the hole again.

'You're mad!' said Tom.

Stella popped the polo into her mouth and grinned as her ears started tingling. 'Well then, I suppose we'll just have to go down on our own - won't we?'

~

Being the oldest and the largest Stella went first, grasping tightly onto the rusty rungs and holding her torch between her teeth. Tom followed, awkwardly clutching his trowel and not daring to look down. His binoculars were slung across him like a satchel.

'You okay, Tom?' Stella's strange whisper, on account of the torch in her mouth, echoed eerily up the hole like a toothless ghost's.

'Fine!' he lied in a squeak.

Stella had been counting each step as she descended. When she reached eighteen she stopped, took the torch from her mouth, and called up.

'Hey, Tom. I've just realised, Harry wouldn't have

been able to get down here on his own!'

'That's just was I was thinking!' said Tom. 'Weird!'

Stella, meanwhile, had dangled one foot down, but couldn't feel any more rungs below her. 'I think we've reached the end,' she called, continuing to splay her leg out in the darkness like a tentacle. Suddenly her foot hit something hard and wide that she was able to rest on. As she pointed her torch down, the tiny beam of light bounced off what looked like the branch of a tree. And then she saw that the wall of the tunnel below the last ladder rung was no longer earthen - it looked like tree bark.

'Tom, I think we've found an *underground tree*!' she yelled. Carefully, she let go of the last rung of the ladder and grasped a couple of short nodules that were sticking out like giant nail-ends from the bark. Dangling one of her feet still lower, she found another branch to rest on.

Soon she discovered there were nodules protruding from all over the place between the branches, making it easy to keep climbing down. 'Follow me, it's okay!' she called. Neither of them had noticed, but the surrounding darkness was turning dim grey.

After they had descended a little farther Stella stopped.

'I don't believe this Tom! We're coming to the outside!' she shrieked. A pool of light was shining up from below and, as they continued descending, daylight began to surround them.

15

'Are we in Australia?' shouted Tom hopefully.

'No idea!' shouted Stella, who could now hear the birds singing.

The branches now began thinning out and soon there were only the nodules of the tree trunk left to step and grasp onto. The sun-drenched grass below looked soft, so Stella jumped the final couple of metres down. Then, as she raised herself from the ground, brushing earth and tiny stones from her knees, she looked up to see the most beautiful lake, surrounded by crimson pink flowering bushes, stretching away in front of her.

Thud! Tom, complete with binoculars and trowel, landed beside her.

'Told you there was water nearby!' said Stella triumphantly, pointing at the lake.

Tom, still breathless, clapped his binoculars to his eyes. 'Where on *earth* are we?' he whispered, scanning from left to right trying to see beyond the trees on the far side. Suddenly he fixed on something moving on the lake. 'Look at that, Stell!'

'*My* goodness!' she murmured. About half way across the lake, a boy in a small boat was rowing frantically in their direction. Stella snatched the binoculars from Tom to get a closer look, almost throttling him.

The boy in the boat didn't see them at first because his back was square onto them as he rowed. However, as he drew closer he turned and spotted them. As soon as he hit the bank he clambered out and began to pull the boat high up in the direction of the tree.

'Gi's a hand wi' this will yer!'

Tom and Stella who had only been able to stand and gawp stepped obediently forward and helped him pull the boat right up under their tree. They were speechless, and all the time couldn't take their eyes off his dirt-smudged face, his ragged brown suit with half-length trousers, and his filthy lace-up ankle boots.

'Naa, don't you go tellin' on me will yer - yer never saw me, right!' he growled.

Despite his snarl, the boy looked terrified. Stella and Tom shook their heads then stood in silence as he dashed into the woodland behind.

'Where did he come from?' whispered Tom.

'More to the point, where's he going?' said Stella. 'Did you see the clothes he was wearing?'

Tom started sniggering. Stella, meanwhile, was staring out across the lake to the far bank in front of the woods where there was a little opening. 'Quick! Give me those binoculars back!'

Tom passed them over and Stella clapped them to her eyes.

'What is it?'

'Oh, no, it's, nothing,' Stella said vacantly. But then as she passed the binoculars back she squinted across the lake again. 'Funny, though, I could have sworn I saw some moles just then!'

'Moles don't come out in daytime, silly!' said Tom.

'Trees don't grow underground!' retorted Stella. 'Now, come on, let's row over!'

5 - The Children in the Garden

The boat slid easily back down the bank and Stella held it steady as Tom clambered in. 'One oar each!' she commanded climbing in after him. Tom took the left and Stella the right. Their recent family trip to the boating lake in Hyde Park quickly paid off, and they soon worked up a rhythm.

'Where do you think we are, Stell?' Tom was marvelling at the deep crimson reflections in the water which shattered into pieces as the oars smashed down into them.

'I haven't the faintest idea,' she said, 'but we'll soon find out! This is the best fun I've had since our first day in Hong Kong! Hannah'll *never* believe it!' All the time Stella was looking over her shoulder watching the distant bank draw closer. 'Nearly there!' The oars were starting to feel heavy. At two metres from the bank they stopped rowing and let the boat drift slowly in. Stella's heart raced as they clambered out and pulled the boat clear of the water. Whatever lay beyond was blocked from view by a small wood, but she had already caught the sound of children's voices on the breeze. A narrow path had been cut through the trees, but she decided it was safer not to use it.

'Follow me!' Stella struck into the woods like a Sergeant Major. Tom pursued, his trowel clutched at his chest, ready for combat. The cool of the woods brought welcome relief; they had both worked up a sweat and Tom's mouth was parched. Crack, crackle, snap - they continued walking for several minutes. Finally, a curtain of light ahead indicated a clearing.

'We're nearly through,' whispered Stella.

'I'm thirsty!' said Tom.

'*Shhh!*' Stella stopped suddenly as the sound of children's chatter floated towards them from somewhere beyond the clearing ahead. She frowned, then nodded them on. The chatter continued as they crept out through the edge of the wood and into the sunlight.

'*There* are the children - through there!' she whispered, pointing through a rhododendron bush. Tom knelt beside Stella and peered through. Beyond a cluster of tree trunks he spotted two young girls sitting on the lawn with a lady wearing a hat tied under her chin. Judging by how strangely they were dressed the children looked as though they might be going to a fancy dress party.

'*LOOK!* THERE'S HARRY!' shouted Tom, jumping up. Harry was streaking across the lawn towards the children and the lady.

'There you are, Harry!' called the smaller girl.

'Who was that?' demanded the older one, looking round.

'You stupid idiot! They've heard us!' Stella snapped in a whisper.

Harry, on hearing Tom's voice, sped past the children and came hurtling through the trees yapping loudly.

'Harry, boy!' Tom tried to catch the tip of the dog's wagging tail, one of Harry's favourite games, and began having so much fun trying to outwit him he didn't notice Stella's sudden silence. 'Hey, Stell, now we know where he goes to!' Tom looked up, but Stella wasn't listening. Instead she was standing face to face with two girls dressed in bright purple party dresses, complete with embroidered patterns around the neckline and a white lace trim at the knee. The girls, who both had beautifully groomed hair – one blonde and one dark - falling in ringlets to their shoulders and decorated with matching purple ribbons, couldn't take their eyes off Stella who, by contrast, looked quite a sight in her sky blue T-shirt, cropped skinny jeans and bright blue plimsolls.

Tom picked up a stick and threw it. Harry ran off again.

'Who are you?' demanded the taller girl, in a grand voice. She was clearly the older of the two and her blonde ringlets glistened importantly in the afternoon sun. 'And, what's more, how do you know Harry?' Stella didn't answer. Instead she fixed her stare on the girls' black woollen tights and shiny black shoes. How strange that they should be wearing clothes like that on a day like this in a park! Perhaps they were royalty – maybe lost princesses or something?

Suddenly a woman's voice was calling.

'Sophie, Emma, come back now, there's good girls! We must finish your lesson before tea.'

'*Lesson?*' said Tom, indignantly. 'Why are you having a lesson in the school holidays?'

'What are you talking about, stupid boy!' snapped the blonde-haired girl.

The dark-haired girl, who looked friendlier, and was obviously her sister, edged forward and smiled. Her large brown eyes sparkled with enthusiasm. 'Mama says the more we learn when we're young, the better off we'll be in society.'

At that moment the rhododendron bush trembled violently and the woman with the hat burst into the clearing. Stella and Tom's eyes drew like magnets onto her long-sleeved dark green dress that swept across the ground like a curtain, and which squeezed her waist so tightly it looked as if it must hold her breath in permanently.

'My goodness! *Who* have we here?' she asked gently. 'A girl in trousers! Well I thought I'd seen it all!' Tom frowned and clutched tightly onto his trowel.

'What's your name?' blurted out the dark-haired younger girl, smiling at Stella.

'Emma, dear, it's rude to ask someone's name without introducing yourself first,' said the lady.

'Sorry, Miss Walker.' She turned to Stella again with a friendly smile. 'How do you do? My name's Emma Gladstone. I'm ten. And that's my sister, Sophie – she's twelve. What's your name please?'

Stella shook her bedraggled blonde hair off her face. She was determined not to appear nervous. 'Stella. I'm eleven. This is my brother Tom. He's eight.'

'I'll be eleven quite soon!' said Emma.

'Not for another month actually!' sneered Sophie.

'That's quite enough, Sophie!' said Miss Walker. She crouched down in front of Tom and Stella. 'But, dears, where are you from? Is your mama or papa here with you?' Stella felt her cheeks start to burn and began to get a sick feeling in her tummy. She gripped her right wrist, feeling with her thumb for her friendship bracelet. But it wasn't there.

'Why are you wearing those funny clothes?' demanded Sophie. 'And what's *that* thing?' She was pointing at Stella's iPhone which was poking out of her jeans pocket.

Miss Walker stood up and rounded on her.

'Sophie, this is your last warning for rudeness! I really don't want to have to tell your mama!'

'I know!' shrieked Emma, suddenly jumping with delight.

'You're my best friend Lucy Cuthbertson's cousins from Australia – aren't you? Your father was the Governor, wasn't he? She *told* me you were moving back!'

She eyed them hopefully as everyone paused for thought. Tom started to open his mouth, but something stirred in Stella.

'That's right!' she cut in. Then she delivered Tom such a piercing glare that he swallowed his words on the spot.

6 - The Boy Thief

'Oh well now, how exciting! Do come and have a cool drink with us!' said Miss Walker. At the mention of fluid Tom perked up again. 'I'm sure the girls would love to hear all about Australia. Do you have a governess over there?' They all trooped out onto the lawn.

'A governess? Oh, yes!' Stella fixed another glare on Tom. Tom, his thoughts focused on cold juice, nodded solemnly.

As they all helped Miss Walker move the rug and a pile of leather bound books into the shade of a tree, Stella found herself glancing at the row of houses on the far side of the lawn.

'Is there something wrong?' said Sophie suddenly.

'*Hey*, there's our house!' shouted Tom, pointing.

'What are you talking about?' said Sophie. 'That's *our* house!'

Stella laughed and quickly shook her head. 'Don't be silly, Tom. Our house is in Australia!' She then clenched her teeth and gave poor Tom such a fierce look he thought he would burst into tears.

'So, Australia!' Miss Walker smiled as she handed round glasses of fruit juice poured from a jug under the tree. 'What's it *really* like over there?' Tom looked at the ground in bewilderment. Stella felt her cheeks start to burn again. Try as she might, all she could picture was the shape of Australia, which she knew resembled a dog's head.

'Well...' she faltered. An image of the Sydney Opera House popped uninvited into her head just as shouts came sailing across the lawn from the direction of the houses. They all looked up to see a man in a dark uniform and hat running towards them, closely followed by another man wearing rolled-up shirt sleeves and braces. A little farther behind came an elegant blonde-haired lady in a long yellow skirt and beautiful white blouse.

'You all right, Miss?' wheezed the man in the uniform looking all around. Miss Walker stood up in a fluster. 'Only there's been another theft. Crawley 'ere saw a young ruffian in the garden, but 'e got away. Looks like 'e's run off with some silver. Mrs Gladstone's coin purse is missin' too. She's in a right state.'

The man called Crawley arrived panting. He immediately narrowed his dark eyes at Tom. 'A good beatin', that's what he'll get when I catch 'im!'

Tom felt his stomach twist into a knot.

Finally, the beautiful woman caught up.

'Sophie! Emma! Thank goodness you're all right!'

'Mama!' shrieked Emma jumping up with Sophie. Sophie and Emma's mother flung her arms around her two children while Stella marvelled at her flowing skirt and elaborate hair arrangement. The man in the dark uniform glanced down at Tom and Stella then back at Miss Walker.

'It's a young lad we're after, about this one's age.' He eyed Tom again. Tom swallowed hard and tried to look angelic.

'My goodness, *who* are these children, Miss Walker?' said Mrs Gladstone. Immediately she freed Sophie and Emma from her grasp.

'They're Lucy Cuthbertson's cousins from Australia, and I guessed first!' said Emma triumphantly. 'She told me they might be coming. I didn't know it would be so soon!'

'Well I never! I've never seen anything like it in my life!' said Mrs Gladstone, peering down her nose. 'If that's how they dress their children in Australia then all I can say is–'

'Look, I'm sorry to interrup', ma'am. But if we want to catch this thief–'

'Oh, yes, of course, do carry on, constable.' The policeman (for it was now obvious that this is what the man in uniform was) knelt down.

'Now, this is important, an' especially for you nippers.' He looked at each of the children in turn, as if trying to see inside their tiny minds. 'Did any of yer see a boy in the gardens in the last hour? Looks kinda scruffy. Tatty brown clothes.'

Tom leaned forward, about to say something, then felt Stella's sharp finger in his ribs. The children solemnly shook their heads in turn as the policeman counted round them again. 'Looks like 'e probably got away,' he grumbled, standing up.

Mrs Gladstone gathered up her skirt and shot a cold glance at Miss Walker. 'Children, I'd like you inside please!' she said. 'I never did have much to say for studying in the garden, and we can't have you out here with a ruffian roaming the grounds, can we?' The children's faces dropped. So, Stella noticed, did Miss Walker's. 'Constable, I count on you to give the place a thorough search - twice over. Crawley, you go too.'

'Yes, ma'm.' Crawley bowed his head. The policeman delivered Mrs Gladstone an icy smile, then headed off into the gardens with Crawley in his wake.

'Well now, what are you two waiting for?' snapped Mrs Gladstone. Tom and Stella scrambled to their feet. 'Go on then! Off you go now, back to Lucy's. And if I were you I'd ask that mother of hers to lend you some half-decent clothes. You certainly can't be seen out in London dressed like that!'

Constance Gladstone then turned and marched off across the lawn with her children and their governess trotting behind, like sorry puppies.

7 – The Time Tunnelers

The moment they were out of sight Tom turned on Stella. Tears of frustration clouded his eyes. 'That *is* our house!' he said crossly. Why did you go and say we live in Australia? I'm going to tell mum!' He lurched forward as quickly as Stella tugged him back.

'Tom, listen,' she said firmly, 'you're forgetting something aren't you? The lake? The hole we climbed down? Don't you see?' Tom looked bewildered. Stella paused, trying to think of how to make him understand. She took in a deep breath. 'Tom, look, I *do* think that is our house, but, well, not at the moment. Look, don't ask me how, but that tunnel we found seems to have taken us back to our garden in past time. That's why everyone's wearing those funny clothes!'

'You're bonkers!' said Tom.

'No I'm not!' said Stella. 'I think the boat you dug up in our garden came from *this* time - I think it's the one we rowed across the lake on today! Our garden must have had a lake that dried up!'

Tom, who had started chipping with his trowel at the bark of the tree, stopped what he was doing and slowly turned to Stella. 'Wow!' he said brightly, his brown eyes almost doubled in size. 'We're really *in the past*? That's *so* cool!' He then gave his big sister the biggest of grins.

Stella, who was thinking what a fantastic adventure this was, put her arm around Tom and kissed his cheek. 'Come on, let's go home. We'll come back another time.'

Moments later they were heading back through the woods towards the lake, sucking on fruit polos and laughing about the ladies' ridiculous long skirts.

'I wonder what happened to Harry?' said Tom, as they retraced their path.

'I wonder where that boy we saw's gone?' said Stella. 'He must be the thief!' And she sucked thoughtfully on her sweet.

To Stella's relief the little boat was still there when they emerged onto the lake bank. Tom sat opposite her peering towards the far side through his binoculars as she rowed them back. He was starting to feel hungry, and they had left their lunch boxes by the log up on the mound.

'You first,' said Stella. They stood at the foot of the tree they had come down. Stella gave Tom a leg up and he quickly grasped onto a nodule and started climbing. Stella followed him up into the shade of the vast branches.

'Where you two goin'? They after you too?' bellowed

a voice from below. Stella was so startled, she nearly lost her footing. Clinging on tightly, she looked down to see the scruffy young boy staring up at her.

'Keep going, Tom!' she called, glancing back up. 'It's the boy who stole the silver – they'll be coming for him!'

Immediately Tom started scrambling more quickly up through the dense branches above. Stella quickly followed.

Higher and higher they went, all the time expecting the darkness to envelop them. But the tunnel didn't appear. All they could see was clear blue sky filtering through the last remaining branches above.

Stella's heart sank. 'Tom! The tunnel's not here. We'd better go down,' she called, trying not to sound scared.

Thud! Stella landed beside the boy who was sitting with his back up against the side of the tree. Thud! Down came Tom, binoculars, trowel and all.

'So,' said the boy, smiling, 'looks likes we's all in trouble!' He paused, briefly, as he looked them up and down. Then he pulled the funniest of faces. 'What them outfits you wearin' then? You from a circus, or what?'

'*We're* not in any trouble, thanks! *You* are!' said Stella sharply. She didn't trust this thief one little bit and clung tightly to her iPhone in case he tried to steal it.

'I'm hungry,' said Tom. 'I wish we'd brought our lunch boxes, Stell.'

''Ere you go lad!' The boy reached into a paper bag

beside him and held out a large hunk of white bread.

'How do we know that's not poisonous!' said Stella. 'You are a thief after all. They told us all about you in the garden!'

The boy sighed 'I never stole nothin'!'

'Yes you did!' said Stella. 'You took some silver! It's lucky they didn't arrest us!'

The boy slowly shook his head. 'It ain't true,' he said wearily.

Stella frowned at him suspiciously.

'Look. Sit down will yer. An' let that boy 'ave sumɪnet ter eat. There's loads 'ere and we ain't goin' no-where 'til the sun goes down. I'm Jack by the way. Nice ter meet yer!'

Despite what she'd heard, Stella couldn't help liking Jack after all. He had a warm smile and friendly brown eyes, and, most importantly, he seemed concerned about Tom.

Soon they were all chewing on the soft white bread and listening to the chatter of the birds in the trees.

'So why do they say you stole something if you didn't?' asked Stella.

Jack shook his head slowly, then started to explain. How his father, Jacob, had been one of the builders of the houses in the garden, and afterwards did regular building work for the Gladstones and the other houses in the garden. How, one day, after some silver went missing in the house, he was falsely accused of stealing by one of the servants and sent to jail. How he was now free, but was a broken man with no-one to recommend him and without any of his work tools which he'd kept in the Gladstones' cellar. Finally, how he, Jack, had snuck into the house to try to retrieve his father's tools to help him.

'Pa lives fer 'is work,' said Jack. 'An' without it I don't think he'll go on much longer. He'll die of a broken mind or else hunger, that's for sure. An' if it ain't that we'll all end up in the workhouse - an' I wouldn't wish that on anyone.'

The children sat in silence. Stella held her knees and stared at the ground. She felt terrible for having called Jack a thief.

'Anyways,' Jack went on, 'that's when I sees Crawley stealin' silver from the Gladstones!'

Tom frowned suspiciously. 'That horrid man we met in the garden?'

'You *saw* Crawley take the silver?' said Stella.

'Sure as I can be,' said Jack. 'See, I'd snuck inter the kitchen through the garden door ter get ter the cellar, when I 'eard someone comin'. So I slips up the back stairs an' immediately spots Crawley acting funny comin' from one o' the rooms. Looked like he was carrying summet under 'is jacket. 'E never saw me, but 'e disappeared right quick down ter the garden. Saw 'im with me own eyes from the balcony window up there.'

Jack described how he'd gone to look for Crawley in

the garden and how, within minutes, half the household was chasing across the garden calling him a thief.

'How did you manage to escape?' asked Tom, his eyes widening.

Jack started to smile. 'Now there's a story! I was runnin' towards the trees when all of a sudden I sees the moles me pa told me about. An' I swear it was just that moment when them folk stopped chasin' me! They thought they'd lost me, but I weren't that far ahead! That's why I decides to row over – jus' ter be on the safe side.'

'Moles? What do moles have to do with anything?' said Stella, frowning.

'I'm not sure,' said Jack, 'but I knows they's special.' He sat up straight and smiled proudly. 'It was pa who discovered 'em – on the firs' day they set to preparing yon' land for buildin'. Whole place was shrouded in mist. Then, out o' the blue 'e sees these moles scuttling in a circle not fifty feet away, near a group of trees.'

Tom and Stella stared at Jack in astonishment.

Jack went on. 'Course when pa told everyone else, they all said 'e was mad. Moles don't come out in the daylight 'n all. An' they certainly don't run round in circles neither! Everyone made a joke of it, but 'e knew they meant summet special. Carried on seein' 'em right up ter when Gladstone threw 'im out.'

'Jack, *I've* seen the moles too!' said Stella excitedly. 'I saw them through Tom's binoculars when we came down the tree. I thought I was imagining it!'

'And *I* saw them in our garden when we first went looking for Harry,' chipped in Tom. '*And* just before we found the tunnel! I thought I was dreaming, Stell!'

Jack looked confused. '*Your* garden? A tunnel? What you talkin' about?'

Stella hesitated for a moment then took a deep breath. She somehow knew that she could trust Jack. 'It's a bit hard to explain, Jack,' she said. 'And I don't really understand what's happened. But, well, you see, Tom and I, we're not from this time. We're from a time in the future - the next century actually - and we live in the Gladstones' house there.'

Jack opened his mouth to say something, but the words carried on tumbling out of Stella's.

'Oh - except it's not one house any more. It's been divided into flats – and we live on the lower ground and raised ground floors. But we do still have the same shared gardens – minus this lake, that is. It's all dried up in our time.' She gave Jack a very broad grin, hoping it would help ease the shock.

'You kiddin' me or what?' said Jack with a look of disbelief.

'Stell's telling the truth,' said Tom eagerly. 'And when we were looking for our neighbour's dog we found a tunnel with a ladder that brought us here! And just before that I saw some moles!'

Jack sat shaking his head.

'Hey! I wonder if the *moles* make the tunnel appear?' said Stella suddenly. 'Actually that makes sense doesn't it? Moles tunnel holes, don't they? Your father must be right, Jack! They *are* special!'

'Jeepers!' said Jack, smiling and shaking his head, 'ain't nothin' gonna surprise me no more after this! Nippers travellin' back through a time tunnel 'n all! Can't wait ter see pa's face when I tell 'im this!'

Tom was beaming from ear to ear. But Stella was suddenly looking serious. She shifted awkwardly where she sat. 'There is one slight problem though,' she said. 'The tunnel's disappeared - that's why we came back down.' She pushed her hair behind her ears and studied her feet. 'I suppose we'll just have to wait for the moles to appear again to make it come back, don't you think?'

In fact, Stella was terrified that the moles would never return, and that she and Tom would be stuck in the past forever, but she wasn't going to let on.

'Must be,' said Jack quickly, 'must be.' He seemed to sense her fear. 'An' seein' them moles looked after me I'm sure they'll look after you two. Anyways, I'll wait with yer both 'til they come – I ain't goin' back over there in no hurry!'

Stella, relieved, began smiling.

Jack leaned towards her, peering at her iPhone. 'So while we's waitin' what's that thing hangin' out yer pocket then?'

36

'Here, try it!' Stella switched on some music and passed it over. As she placed the earphones into Jack's ears his smudged brown face expanded with delight.

'Jeepers!' he shouted. 'You got people in 'ere or what? Aa d'ya do that then?'

His eyes grew wider and wider in disbelief, as his mouth fell wide open. And as the sun finally set behind the trees, Stella and Tom fell about in fits of laughter.

8 - A Moonlight Raid

Over two hours had passed and the light was fading fast. Tom had fallen asleep under the tree and Jack and Stella had been lazing on the bank of the lake describing life in their own times. The last of Stella's polos had gone.

'The moles better come soon,' said Stella, anxiously.

'I'll stay with yer 'til they do, like I said,' said Jack. 'But we'll 'ave ter go over fer some supplies if they ain't 'ere by nightfall. I wasn't countin' on usin' up me bread and that littlun's gonna need summet more before long.'

Stella's heart began to race.

'To the house?' she whispered.

'Course!'

Jack reached inside his ankle boot and pulled out a large key.

'Wow! Where did you get that?' said Stella.

'I 'borrowed' it from me pa, didn't I?' said Jack with a wide grin. 'It's the kitchen back door key. Gladstone forgot ter get it off 'im when 'e threw 'im out - an' the kitchen leads to the cellar where the tools are!' He chuckled under his breath. 'Anyways, I'm sure there's plenty in that kitchen fer all of us!'

Stella beamed back at Jack. His confidence was reassuring, and all her worries about being stuck in past time had disappeared.

'Can we go and see my room?' Tom said eagerly, when he finally awoke. Jack laughed out loud.

'No ways!' he said and shook his head.

Stella's watch read exactly 1.30 when they rowed across the lake under the light of a full moon. Whatever time it was here, she concluded it was probably 1.30 in the afternoon at home: she certainly didn't feel tired, and her stomach was only now starting to rumble. The boat drifted in, and as they entered the woods she switched on her orange torch which Jack spent five minutes studying from all angles and beaming around in the trees.

'This is a fancy little flashlight!' he said with a wide smile. 'Sure ain't seen one like this before!'

'You can take it when we leave!' promised Stella.

Stella squeezed Tom's hand tightly as they approached a large door which, in their own flat, was the double French door leading from the sitting room to the patio garden. Jack pulled the key from his boot and, seconds later, they slipped quietly in.

As Stella switched on her torch again it illuminated not a living room at all, but a large kitchen. The narrow shaft of light beamed slowly around the room, revealing an enormous fireplace piled high with logs, and an array of jugs and kettles sitting in its hearth. Next to the fireplace stood a large black iron double stove, and on the opposite side of the room, two rectangular sinks, each with a single tap. In the centre of the room stood a long wooden pine table, and from the ceiling there hung so many pots and pans that it looked more like a cooks' shop than a kitchen.

Stella and Tom stood speechless.

'This way!' whispered Jack urgently. At the far end of the room he opened a solid wooden door that led them into an enormous walk-in pantry. ''Ere's where they keep the food - 'elp yerselves, but be quick!'

Tom's hungry eyes feasted on a large fruit cake which had a couple of slices taken from it.

'Go on, 'ave some!' said Jack with a nod. Tom reached up and pulled a chunk of cake away and stuffed it into his mouth. Stella, meanwhile, found a lump of cheese under a dish, and some more bread in a wicker basket. She took a bite of the cheese then tied the rest inside Tom's treasure rag while Jack stuffed apples and pears into his pockets.

'This'll do!' Jack whispered sharply. 'Let's go!'

But Tom, with his tummy satisfied, had other ideas.

'I'm not going until I see my room!' he murmured solemnly.

Stella fixed her torch beam and a nasty glare on him. 'Tom,' she whispered crossly, 'do you want us to get caught?'

'I don't care!' he muttered through clenched teeth.

Seeing his arms folded, an unblinking gaze and both feet planted squarely on the ground, Stella knew they were onto a lost cause. 'Jack, can we show him?' she pleaded in a whisper. 'He won't leave if we don't.'

Jack shook his head and smiled. 'Your littlun's got nerve. I likes that! Let's go then, but be *qui*et!'

Jack led the way through a door that Tom and Stella didn't recognise from their own home, but soon they found themselves climbing a familiar staircase towards the front door. The walls of the main hallway were adorned with large heavily framed paintings whose subject matter Stella couldn't make out. Jack was now heading for another set of stairs she didn't recognise. Stella darted forward and tugged at his sleeve, then pointed at the door beside her.

'This ain't a bedroom!' he whispered.

Stella nodded vigorously then pointed at Tom. Jack gave a puzzled frown. The door was ajar and creaked so loudly when they pushed it open that they all froze. Nothing stirred, except the hollow tick of a clock somewhere in the hallway above.

Quietly, they stepped inside and Stella switched on her

torch. As the beam lit up the room, Tom's mouth fell open. His bedroom was in fact a dining room - and one fit for kings and queens at that! In the centre of the room, which spanned the width of both his and Stella's bedrooms, was a vast mahogany dining table complete with three sets of silver candelabras, spaced evenly in a line down the middle. The table was surrounded by about twenty crimson velvet high backed chairs, and above it hung an enormous chandelier which shimmered silently in the moonlight filtering in through the shutters. A vast and elaborate gilt-framed mirror hung over what was, of course, *his* fireplace, which stood at one end of the table. Either side of the fireplace, and on all the other walls, huge portraits of the Gladstone family looked down on them.

'*Look over there!*' whispered Stella, giggling under her hand. Tom looked across to see a portrait of a young girl with a puppy on her lap. A small plaque at the bottom read 'E. M. Gladstone'.

'That's Emma and Harry!' whispered Tom.

Tom and Stella had just completed a silent circuit of the room when a distant floorboard creaked. Stella snapped off her torch.

'Quick!' whispered Jack, turning for the door. But it was too late. The footsteps quickened across the hallway above towards the top of the stairs. Jack glanced around in desperation. His eyes rested on the fireplace. 'Up 'ere!' he whispered darting across the room. 'Do as I say, and don't breathe a word!' Jack ducked his head under and up inside the chimney breast. Tom and Stella followed. 'Feel up high. There's a ledge. Now, cling on an' pull yer feet onto them bricks stickin' out. I'll 'elp the littlun.'

Stella reached for the ledge and pulled herself up inside the chimney breast, resting her feet on the bricks below which jutted out just out of sight of the room. Jack, meanwhile, hoisted Tom up and soon all three were clinging to the inside of the dark chimney flue while occasional clouds of soot dusted down on them.

The footsteps drew nearer, and as they all looked down a dim light ebbed into the hearth below before slowly fading away, along with the sound of the steps.

'Fiddle! 'E's gone down!' whispered Jack. 'We're gonna 'ave ter wait 'ere 'til 'e comes up. An' if 'e's goin' fer summet ter eat we're all done for!'

Whoever it was downstairs was taking a long time going about their business. Stella, bored with waiting, flicked on the torch, almost making everyone fall into the fireplace.

'One o' pa's chimneys. Nice brickwork, eh?' whispered Jack proudly. Stella beamed the light up the narrow flue. 'Shine the light over there will yer!' Stella obliged. 'There it is! 'J' fer Jacob. That's me pa's sign. Always in the same place.'

Tom, ever thoughtful, had an idea. 'Can I write my name?' he whispered eagerly.

''Ere, you's a clever nipper, you is! Use this!' Jack

pulled out the house key and passed it over. Tom dug hard into the brickwork, and had soon engraved a lopsided letter 'T'.

'Someone's coming!' whispered Stella, clicking off the torch. Tom slipped the key into his pocket and grasped back onto the ledge. They all glanced down, holding their breath, as the fireplace was once again flooded with orange light. Tom, who was suddenly starting to sweat, wasn't sure he could hang on much longer. Soot dust covered his hair, his eyelashes, and his nose which now began to twitch with a sneeze. Already his grip was loosening, but he was determined not to be the one to let them down. Then, one final twitch and–

'Lucy! Stella! Tom! Are you in here?' A child's urgent whisper cut across the darkness.

Tom's sneeze evaporated just at the moment his foot slipped and his grip on the ledge gave way. Crash! Down he landed in a heap in the fireplace where he found himself nose to toe with a small pink foot. Slowly, he stuck his head out. The foot belonged to Emma.

'Tom!' she gasped, cupping her hand around her candle. 'What *are* you doing up our chimney?' Tom scrambled out, amidst clouds of black soot which quickly found a home on her long white night gown. Emma gave him a broad grin.

'Stella's here!' he whispered excitedly. 'And Jack!'
'*Jack?*'

Just then four feet dangled down into the fireplace;

two wearing bright blue plimsolls, two clad in tatty brown lace-up ankle boots.

'That's Jack!' said Tom, pointing at the boots and giggling.

Stella and Jack jumped down and emerged dusted with soot. Emma stepped back a pace, her candle flickering violently.

'It's the boy thief!' she squeaked. 'What are *you* doing here? And what are you doing with Lucy's cousins? You stole our silver – and mama's beautiful coin purse, you mean boy!'

'Emma, it's not like that,' whispered Stella politely. 'We came to get food. Please, let me explain about Jack.'

'How did you know we were here?' said Tom, frowning.

Emma smiled proudly. 'I saw you come across the lawn, of course! And by the way, you left your binoculars on the table downstairs, silly!'

Tom gulped and studied his shoes.

'Anyway,' she said, straightening her back, 'if I'd have known you had the boy thief with you I'd have woken mama and papa. I thought you were with your cousin Lucy coming on a mole hunt!'

'Jeepers, yer knows about the moles 'n all!' blurted out Jack. Emma threw him a nervous glance.

'So, what's it got to do with you?' she demanded.

'Emma,' whispered Stella, 'we all know about the moles. Do you know they have special powers?'

45

Emma frowned suspiciously.

'You see, Emma, Tom and I aren't really from Australia, we're from *another time*! And Jack didn't steal from your family. It was Crawley!'

Emma's candle flickered violently again. Then, very slowly, her eyes began to widen. She opened her mouth and took the deepest of breaths while Stella, Tom and Jack all froze, waiting for her to scream.

9 - The Dance of the Moles

'I *knew it!*' she squealed. 'I *knew* it! I *told* Lucy the moles must have special powers, but she didn't believe me! And I'm glad to hear you're not the thief, Jack, otherwise I'd have to call papa!' She gave him a sweet smile then gathered up her night gown. 'But quick. I'd better get you out of here. Papa might wake and there's soot everywhere!'

It was half past two by Stella's watch as they emerged into the moonlight. Emma had slipped on a pair of ankle boots and donned an extremely fine looking coat over her night dress.

'Tell me more about the moles,' she said, brushing back her dark ringlets as they trooped across the lawn towards the trees.

'Well, what does yer know already?'

'Not much, except I've seen them loads of times from my bedroom window in the night - all scuttling in a circle in the moonlight. At first I thought it was a dream, but finally I told Lucy about them and we planned a mole hunt for tonight, except she's forgotten of course. Dear, silly Lucy!'

They all sat down under a tree out of sight of the houses and tucked into the food. Between them they told Emma about the time tunnel, about Jack's father being wrongly accused and Jack coming to get his tools, and about Crawley acting suspiciously in the drawing room.

'Oh dear, Jack. I am sorry. Papa can be so beastly sometimes. So you think Crawley took the silver?' Jack nodded solemnly. Emma frowned deeply. 'You know I've always thought there was something strange about him. I told Sophie, but of course she said it was just my childish imagination. Sophie can be such a *bore* sometimes!' She shook her head disapprovingly.

'Don't you go worryin' about what yer sister says!' said Jack, laughing. 'She obviously ain't one of the chosen few!'

'What do you mean by that?' Emma gave Jack a puzzled look.

'Well,' said Jack, 'looks like the moles on'y appears for some folk – an' it looks like *we's* the ones who's extra special round 'ere!'

'They must have appeared for Harry too!' piped up Tom.

'What's Harry got to do with this?' said Emma quickly.

'Everything!' said Stella smiling. 'He's why we came here in the first place!'

'*My* Harry?' said Emma, sitting back.

'Emma, does Harry ever... *go missing*?' said Stella slowly.

Immediately Emma's face lit up. 'Oh, all the time! Mama finds it so tiresome. But he always comes back, without fail! Dearest Harry! We were born for each other!'

Stella suddenly kneeled up. '*Look - over there!*' she whispered. They all turned and gazed out to the lawn. Under the silver light of the moon a group of four moles scuttled round and round, forming a tight circle. The children sat transfixed while the moles continued their ritual for about a minute before vanishing right before their eyes.

'Hopefully that means the time tunnel's ready,' said Jack quickly. 'We'd better get goin'. I'll row you over.' They scrambled to their feet.

Emma glanced across at the houses, then quickly back at the children. '*I'm* coming with you!' she said firmly. 'Lucy or no Lucy!'

'Brilliant!' said Stella. 'And *I'll* tell my parents you're a neighbour's niece from Australia and you've come to visit for the day!' Suddenly she realised how much she'd missed having a true friend in her new home. Emma would help fill that gap - and they'd be able to visit each other back and forth.

At that moment a door slammed over by the houses. Within seconds men's voices and the crack of dry twigs underfoot echoed around the garden.

'Emma! Emma! Where are you? Are you out there? Crawley, you go that way!'

'It's papa!' gasped Emma looking terrified. 'Quick! You must go!'

Tom immediately turned and started running towards the woods.

'Emma, darling. Are you out there?' Mrs Gladstone's anxious calls had joined the chorus.

'Come on, Stella, we must go!' said Jack.

'Run, Stella! Go!' Emma's voice was quivering as her eyes filled with tears. 'I'm coming, papa!' she shouted, without moving. 'It was only Harry!'

'Let's *go*, Stella!' said Jack.

Stella stared into Emma's eyes. Was their adventure really ending so soon?

'*Come on will yer!* The tunnel won't wait forever!'

Jack was tugging at Stella's sleeve, and now as his words echoed in her ears she found herself glancing, as if in slow motion, from Emma to a tall figure of a man racing across the lawn towards them.

'You get back! I'll 'ead 'im off!' shouted Jack. And before Stella could react he had pushed past her and dashed out into path of Henry Gladstone.

'It's the boy!' roared Mr Gladstone. 'I'm going after him! Emma's here!'

Stella glanced back at Emma.

'Find the tunnel! Come and see us!' she whispered

holding back her tears, then she turned and ran towards the trees.

Tom and Stella entered the wood breathless. Stella flicked on her torch as they crashed through the branches in a half-run. 'Don't worry, Tom we'll be home soon,' she said panting.

'But what about Jack?' cried Tom, already slowing down. 'We can't leave him - they'll catch him!'

'He'll be fine... He'll hide up a tree,' Stella called uncertainly over her shoulder. Just then a child's pained scream filled the night air and echoed eerily around the treetops.

Tom halted in his tracks. 'That was Jack!' he shouted. 'He's been caught, Stella. Jack's been caught!'

Stella stopped and turned, resting her hand on her chest. Her heart was pounding so heavily she could feel it against her palm. She swallowed hard as she fought back tears. 'There's nothing we can do, Tom,' she said, her voice breaking. 'We *must* go home!'

But Tom had other ideas, and immediately turned and started heading back towards the clearing. Stella raced after him. 'Come back, Tom! *Come back will you!* The tunnel won't wait you know! Do you want to get stuck here *forever?*'

'They'll beat him!' screamed Tom. 'They'll lock him in some horrible child's prison! That's what they do here! We can't leave him, Stell, we can't!'

Stella grabbed Tom's arm and started dragging him backwards. 'Tom! It's too dangerous! If they beat Jack they'll beat us too! *We'll* end up in prison!' Tears were suddenly streaming down her cheeks.

The voices in the garden were drawing nearer.

'Let's go, Tom! Let's go!'

Seconds later they were fleeing through the trees.

The children rowed back in silence. A low mist hung over the water, dampening their downtrodden spirits further. In her mind Stella battled with images of whippings and beatings. Crawley had it in for Jack, of that she was sure. Why oh why had she lingered on the lawn? She sighed deeply, but said nothing. Tom stared despondently at the seat where Jack had sat earlier. They hadn't even had a chance to say goodbye. Slowly he started to sob.

'You first!' said Stella quietly as she gave Tom a leg up to the first nodule on the tree. The higher they climbed, the darker the air all around them became and very soon the dense branches had completely blotted out the light of the moon. Stella flicked on her torch again. Moments later Tom located the first rung of the ladder. And now, as he climbed towards the light source in silence, all he could think about was coming back down and rescuing Jack.

10 - About Turn

Tom and Stella emerged squinting out of the little hole deep inside the bushes. Stella looked at her watch. It was almost 4 o'clock; six hours after they had gone down.

'Look, Tom, our lunch boxes!' She tried to sound cheerful as she peered out towards the log. 'At least mum and dad can't have been out.'

They picked up the lunch boxes and hurried out onto the lawn where the sound of their mother's piano playing danced on the afternoon breeze. A lump rose up in Stella's throat. How abruptly their dream had turned into a nightmare! And now, as she looked all around the garden, she could only imagine how it might have been with Emma there.

Tom stared at the grass in despair. Each step took him further away from the possibility of helping Jack. How could they do this? How could they abandon Jack after he'd been so kind to them? As their garden gate came into view, his heart skipped a beat. He stopped dead. 'But Stella, what about Jack's *father*? He might die if Jack doesn't go back! We've *got* to go back and help him!'

Tears of frustration clouded Stella's eyes. 'Are you mad, Tom? Do you know how lucky we were to get away just then? They'll be searching that garden high and low for us right now! Besides, if the tunnel disappears again *then what*? What about *us*? What about mum and dad?' As she turned and walked towards their gate her heart sank at the hopelessness of it all.

Tom didn't move. All he could hear were Jack's cries echoing inside his head. Then, as if from nowhere, a passion took hold of him and swelled through his body, urging him to turn around and go back. Stella, lost in a world of her own, was almost at their back door.

Tom cupped his hands each side of his mouth and called to his sister. 'JACK RISKED HIS LIFE FOR US, STELL, AND I'M *NOT* GOING TO LEAVE HIM THERE TO DIE!' He turned and started running towards The Island, overcome with a sense of elation. 'IT'S NOW OR NEVER!' he shouted to the treetops. 'IT'S NOW OR NEVER!' Suddenly he didn't care whether Stella was coming - or that other people might hear him. Nor, for that matter, did he care that Charlie Green was giving him one of his strange looks from a distant flowerbed. He must do this. He must do this for Jack - and for Jack's father, Jacob.

Stella reached for the kitchen door handle. 'There it is!' she breathed, spying her friendship bracelet. She swallowed hard as she slipped it off the door handle and onto her wrist. What a perfect present it would have made for Emma! Something she could have travelled back and forth through time with! She knew that Hannah would approve once she'd explained everything – the bracelet would join all three of them across time and distance.

Something made her start. She spun round. Tom had been yelling at her, but she had been so absorbed in her thoughts that she hadn't been listening.

'IT'S NOW OR NEVER!' came an echo through the trees. 'NOW OR NEVER...!'

To her horror she just caught sight of the back of Tom disappearing onto The Island.

It was difficult to see inside the rhododendron bush without Stella's torch and Tom had to scrabble about for several seconds feeling for the hole. For a terrible moment he thought it had gone. But then as his hand slipped over the edge he breathed a deep sigh of relief. He placed his foot down onto one of the ladder rungs and looked out towards the mound.

'It's still here, Stell! It's not too late!' he shouted. He took a deep breath, promised himself he wouldn't be scared by the dark, then slowly started climbing down.

Inside the tunnel Tom could see nothing. He gripped tightly onto each rung, counting each step as he went and watching the dim pool of light disappear above him. He was surprised how quickly he could go. Sixteen, seventeen, eighteen. He swung his foot below and found the first nodule. And now, as he took one last look up towards home, he longed for his sister's company.

Stella raced towards The Island, her heart pounding. What if the tunnel disappeared with Tom inside it? What if he got trapped in the past forever! And whose fault was it, after all, that Jack was stuck in the woods? If she hadn't lingered in the garden none of this would have happened! She dived inside the rhododendron bush and flicked on her torch. Tears blurred her vision as she scrambled across the undergrowth. Tom might be stupid sometimes - and extremely annoying - but how incredibly brave he was!

At first she couldn't remember where the hole was, and as she thumped with her torch on the ground all around her, her cheeks began to burn in terror. Then, just as the first tear broke free and rolled down, her left knee slipped over a ledge and disappeared beneath her.

Slowly and carefully Tom located the first tree nodule, then the next and the next, his sweating body clinging tightly against the tree trunk as he dangled one foot down, rested it, then released his grip on the nodule above him. After a few moments he began to make out shadows. Soon he could see the branches of the tree below him through the faint glimmer of dawn. He jumped the final metres, as before, and landed awkwardly on the soft ground below. Then, as he scrambled up and stared out across the lake his heart sank. He would never make it over on his own.

An eerie yellow light suddenly bounced through the trees and onto the lawn.

'Tom! I'm here!' called Stella in a whisper. And, as Tom looked up to see the outline of his emerging big sister, his mouth curled into a crescent-shaped grin.

'So, you thought you'd row over on your own, did you?' said Stella, smiling. As the oars moved heavily through the water a gentle lapping sound broke the stillness of the night air.

'I could have done it!' said Tom, frowning.

Stella burst out laughing. Tom frowned for about two more seconds then slowly started to giggle.

As they neared the far bank voices echoed in the distance. 'They're still looking for us!' whispered Stella, her heart starting to race again. They clambered out of the boat and walked a short way into the wood. 'Okay,' she said, her voice trembling. 'We're just going to have to wait here 'til everything's died down.'

'Then what?' said Tom anxiously. His hand was sweating as he grasped onto his treasure rag in his pocket.

Stella breathed in deeply and shrugged her shoulders. 'Who knows?'

At that moment Tom felt something cold and metallic between his fingers. It must have been trapped in the folds of his treasure rag. 'Stella!' he gasped pulling the key from his pocket. 'It's the Gladstones' key. I never gave Jack the key back!'

The garden had been quiet for a good half an hour. Finally the children got up and crossed to the line of trees that looked towards the houses. The moon had faded leaving the lawn dull and lifeless. The trees and bushes now stood wrapped in the grey cloak of dawn and as the children peered across, they could see that the house was in darkness, apart from the faintest glimmer of light from a small window high up.

Slowly, they crept across the lawn and into the patio garden. 'I bet that's Emma's window up there!' whispered Stella.

'Maybe she's waiting for us. Maybe it's a sign!' whispered Tom.

'I hope she hasn't fallen asleep!' murmured Stella, twirling the bracelet on her wrist.

The kitchen was in darkness as they peered on tip-toe through the window. Suddenly the silence and the emptiness were too much for Tom. 'It's too late, Stell!' he whispered desperately. 'He's gone! They've taken Jack to the prison!'

'*Oh* no they haven't!' said an excited voice behind them. 'They've tied him all up and locked him in the *cellar*!'

Tom and Stella swung round in terror to find a young

girl standing triumphantly behind them with her hands on her hips and her feet wide apart. She was wearing a long dark coat over ankle length boots.

'Hello,' she said, her eyes doubling in size. '*I'm* Lucy Cuthbertson. Who *on earth* are you?'

11 - Rescue

Lucy had been woken by Mr Gladstone's shouts and had seen everything through the kitchen window.

'Poor Emma! Mr Gladstone gave her a real going over about who'd she'd been with out in the garden. Emma stuck to her story, though. Blamed Harry of course.' Lucy tossed her long blonde hair back behind her shoulder and lifted her chin. 'Of course *I* knew she'd been with someone else!'

'How?' whispered Tom, transfixed.

Lucy sighed impatiently and glanced at her eyebrows. 'Curling her hair around her forefinger of course! Emma *always* does that when she's lying! Anyway, which house are you from? Emma didn't tell me it would be a mole hunting *party!* Otherwise I might have woken up on time!' She gave a quick frown. 'You *still* haven't told me your names by the way!'

'I'm Stella and this is my brother, Tom,' said Stella quickly. 'I'm sorry, Lucy, but we don't have time to explain any more now. It's nearly morning, and if Jack's in the cellar we'd better get in there now, before everyone wakes up again.'

Lucy cocked her head to one side and frowned. 'Who *is* the poor boy, anyway? He's a thief isn't he? What's Emma got to do with him?'

Stella shook her head. 'Lucy, you're just going to have to trust me. You know we're friends of Emma's–'

'I know,' said Lucy brightly.

'Well, Jack's a good friend of hers too. She'll tell you all about it tomorrow, I'm sure.'

Lucy frowned and nodded. 'All right, all right,' she said impatiently. 'But tell me this. Exactly *how* do you propose to get inside?'

'With a key, of course!' said Tom grinning. And as he pulled the key from his pocket Lucy's eyes lit up with delight.

Moments later they stood by the kitchen door waiting to go in. Stella hesitated then quickly turned to Lucy. 'Lucy,' she whispered urgently. 'Please, when we get out of here with Jack you must promise to go straight back to your house. Don't try to follow us. We *must* go our separate ways - otherwise we'll all be caught! Emma will explain, I promise.'

Lucy tossed another glance skywards. 'All right, all right!' she said, with an impatient sigh. 'But do let's *get on* with it for goodness' sake!'

As the key turned, the lock clanked loudly making all

three children jump. For a moment they paused, then slowly crept inside. The remains of a small log burned in the fireplace, giving the air a welcome warmth. Stella reached for her torch, glanced across at Lucy, then thought better of it.

'It's down here!' whispered Lucy. The children crept after her towards the pantry they had stolen food from earlier. Suddenly Lucy stepped to one side and pointed to the floor.

'I've never seen him in such a fury!' she whispered excitedly.

'Who?' said Tom, starting to tremble.

'Crawley of course! He beat him three times across the back, then tied him all up! Said the police could wait 'til dawn and the boy could wait with the rats! Mr Gladstone'll be furious if ever he finds out. But he's gone back to bed of course.'

Stella's stomach felt hollow as she dropped to her knees and felt around in the half-light. Thank goodness Tom had made them come back down. She grasped onto a small handle, then with help of the others managed to pull the door up and open. As it clanked back onto the floor muffled cries rose up from the darkness.

'Hold your breath everyone!' whispered Stella. She glanced nervously at Lucy, then flicked on her torch - to meet Jack's terrified eyes gleaming up at her from where he sat bound and gagged against a wall at the foot of the wooden steps.

'*Jack!*' whispered Stella in horror.

'Where did you get *that!*' gasped Lucy, staring at the torch.

'Australia!' said Tom, raising his eyebrows. He then dived down the stairs to help his friend.

The rag around Jack's mouth was sodden and wet with saliva and it took Tom several seconds to pull it down and around his neck.

''Ow d'yer get in 'ere, then?' said Jack beaming. Through his dirt-smudged face Tom could see that he had been crying. But he didn't let on. Instead he proudly pulled the key from his pocket.

'Get a move on, will you!' whispered Stella crossly.

Tom was now desperately fumbling at Jack's back with the ties around his wrists. 'I can't get them off!' he whispered in panic.

Stella gritted her teeth. 'Pull, Tom, pull!'

Lucy darted into the kitchen and returned a few seconds later holding out the most enormous kitchen knife that glinted in the light thrown up by the torch. 'Try this!' she said proudly.

Stella stared at the knife and swallowed hard. 'I'll do it,' she said quickly. She grasped the knife handle and scrambled down the steps. Tom held the torch steady while Stella cut carefully through the rags and released Jack's hands.

'I won't forget this!' said Jack, flinching slightly. 'Yer's really saved me skin this time.' He grabbed the knife, and in one clean swipe which took the children's breath away he cut his legs free.

'Now,' he said jumping up, 'I thinks it's time we all went *'ome* so ter speak!'

With wide grins Tom and Stella made their way back up the steps behind him.

'Let's go!' whispered Lucy importantly – but then stopped dead as a child's hand holding out a flickering yellow candle appeared in the doorway to the hall.

'Emma!' squealed Stella in delight – just as Sophie stepped into view.

For a split second the children stood staring at one another, no-one daring to breathe. Then Lucy spoke up. 'Why, Sophie!' she said, in a voice as stiff as her grin. 'What *on earth* are you doing up at this time?'

Sophie peered down her nose at Lucy then moved a slow stare from Stella, to Tom, to Jack. Gradually but surely a broad smile spread out across her face. She then heaved her chest, took the deepest of breaths – and yelled at the top of her lungs, '*Crawley! Papa! I've caught them!*'

In an instant the house came alive. Floorboards thumped. Voices shouted. Feet thundered down stairways. 'I'm on me way!' echoed the yell of Crawley.

The children fled past Sophie towards the door, the Gladstones' key clattering across the stone floor as it fell.

'Caught *whom*, Sophie?' said Lucy sarcastically, then dived into the garden after the others.

12 – Guilty

Tom, Jack and Stella tore across the lawn towards The Island, not daring to glance back for fear of slowing themselves. And as they raced through the fading dawn mist, Stella's heart skipped a beat as she glimpsed a group of moles scuttling in a circle by the line of the trees ahead. Her mouth widened into a smile just as her plimsoll struck something hard and she found herself stumbling towards the ground.

As quickly as her hands hit the sodden grass, she pushed herself up to see Jack and Tom disappearing towards the woods and Lucy heading off to the right. A second later she was back on her feet, but then was immediately winded by the grasp of a man's thick arm her around her waist.

'*Gottcha!*' snarled Crawley in triumph. His breath was hot in her ear.

'Get off me!' squealed Stella, gasping. Pummelling furiously with her elbows she tried to break free. But Crawley's grip around her waist continued to tighten and her iPhone was now digging deep into the left side of her tummy through her jeans pocket.

'*Ouch!* You're hurting me! *Get off!*'

As she struggled from side to side she was aware that the others were now running back in her direction.

'*Not* 'til I have the boy thief!' growled Crawley.

'Jack's not a thief!' Stella grunted between clenched teeth. She was pulling forward with all her might, but to no avail.

'Stella's right!' cut in an angry voice from one side. '*You're* the only thief around here, Crawley, and *I'm* going to tell papa!'

Immediately Crawley loosened his grip and Stella looked up in astonishment to see Emma step from the shadows, still wearing her nightgown and overcoat. Tom, Jack and Lucy came to a breathless halt behind her.

Crawley snorted indignantly. 'Well, well, now Miss Emma. Albert Crawley a thief, eh? Who's been telling you that nonsense?'

'You *are* a thief!' said Emma, unwaveringly. 'And *you've* been stealing our silver! *And* mama's money!'

Stella's heart was racing. As she felt her iPhone through her jeans pocket she suddenly had an idea – she knew exactly where to find the record button.

Crawley's breathing paused in her ear. As his grip loosened again, she slipped the phone from her pocket, slid her finger quickly across and tapped twice.

'Well, well, Miss Emma,' he snarled. 'An' jus' s'ppose I

'ad been stealin' your precious silver? Who's gonna believe you anyways.' He narrowed his dark eyes. 'You lot are in enough trouble as it is already, so best keep yer mouths shut fer yer own good!'

At that moment Henry Gladstone burst through the bushes.

'What the blazes is going on, Crawley?' He peered over at Jack. 'And what in heaven's name is that boy still doing here?'

Immediately Crawley freed Stella and stood upright. 'Sir,' he said in a barely recognisable voice. 'It was the boy. He put up a struggle, see. Out of control he was.' He squinted darkly in Jack's direction. 'An' then when he threatened me with a knife I 'ad to lock 'im in the cellar, sir. Just going to fetch the police, I was, sir, when this lot broke in.'

Emma stepped forward, her dark eyes gleaming furiously. 'He's lying papa! He's lying!' She rounded on Crawley. 'Jack's not the thief, Crawley! *You are!* And poor Jacob was never a thief either! Jack's his son and he told us about you accusing him.'

A stunned silence followed, broken only by the somewhat flustered arrival of Mrs Gladstone and Sophie, in the company of two policemen.

'Emma Gladstone, what *are* you saying?' Her father's voice was shaking. 'This is complete and utter nonsense. To suggest that *Crawley–*'

'But, papa, I've got *proof!*' Emma stepped forward

again, and pulled a rolled up cloth from under her coat. The children's eyes all widened.

Crawley shuffled sideways as Henry Gladstone reached out and took the bundle from his daughter. With a bewildered frown he knelt to the ground and unwrapped the cloth, which revealed an assortment of small silver objects.

'Well I never, Constance!' he breathed. 'Here's your pillbox! And here's that salt cellar that went missing, and the jug! No coin purse though. Where is it, Crawley? Spent all the money have you?'

The first policeman stepped forward, quietly positioning himself behind Crawley who ignored Mr Gladstone's question and was starting to shift uncomfortably.

Mrs Gladstone's face was taut and pale. 'Emma, dear,' she said, pulling her shawl around her nightgown, 'where did you find all this stuff?'

'Harry found it for me,' said Emma, her gaze still fixed on Crawley. 'Buried in a hole under a bush.' She narrowed her eyes. 'Buried there because Crawley was trying to hide it!'

Quietly, Stella breathed a sigh of relief.

'Now look 'ere,' said Crawley sharply, making everyone start. 'That silver's got nothin' ter do with me!' He shot a dark look at Jack. 'There's no proof I put it there! It's the boy I tell yer! I saw 'im with me own eyes, taking silver from the house 'e was. An' money 'n all.'

Mr Gladstone, becoming exasperated, stood up shaking his head. 'You know, Emma, Crawley is quite right. A pile of our silver in the garden hardly makes him a thief! I'm afraid to say that if you're going to expound such a ridiculous theory, you're going to have to come up with some proof!'

A smile flickered across Crawley's mouth just as Stella stepped forward, her arm shaking as she slowly held her iPhone out in front of her.

'I've got proof,' she said calmly.

'What in heaven's name is that?' said Henry Gladstone briskly. But as quickly as he reached out to take it, he pulled his hand back as a familiar yet oddly disengaged voice filled the air in front of him.

'Well, well, Miss Emma. An' jus' s'ppose I 'ad been stealin' your precious silver? Who's gonna believe you anyways. You lot are in enough trouble as it is already, so best keep yer mouths shut fer yer own good!'

For a few seconds no-one moved, apart from the first policeman who started furiously scribbling down notes.

'What on earth's *Crawley* doing inside that box?' exclaimed Lucy, saucer-eyed.

Emma gave Stella a triumphant smile, then stamped her foot with excitement.

'You see, papa! I *told* you! I *told* you Crawley was the thief!'

But Mr Gladstone, still staring drop-jawed at the iPhone, didn't answer. Along with his wife and his eldest daughter, he seemed to have gone into a momentary trance.

Crawley started muttering in bewilderment, then took two paces backwards – into the firm grip of the second policeman.

Mr Gladstone finally snapped out of his trance and started slowly shaking his head. 'I'll make this up to Jacob,' he said, 'if it's the last thing I do.'

As Crawley struggled with the policeman Jack smiled and nodded gently at Tom and Stella, then sidled towards a bush.

'Where's that poor boy?' said Mr Gladstone, suddenly looking all around. 'Jacob's son, eh? Well I'll be damned.'

'Musta been frightened off,' said the policeman. 'He won't be far, sir.'

'Well get someone to go and look for him, will you please? We need to clean him up and take him home to his family.'

'Oh, *Lucy*, dear,' said Emma loudly as Crawley was led away. She was staring hard in her friend's direction and curling her hair purposefully around her forefinger. 'Isn't your *uncle's* machine from Australia quite *wonderful*? And to think that he let *your cousins* bring it with them on their *visit* to you!'

As soon as Lucy saw Emma twisting her hair with her fingers, her puzzled frown metamorphosed into a wide smile.

'Oh! Why – yes - *of course*, Emma - it's quite *unbelievable*, isn't it!'

She feigned a yawn and tossed her long blonde hair behind her shoulder. 'Well, *cousins*, I think we're all very tired, aren't we? Time for bed I think!' And she slipped her arms through Tom and Stella's, turned them around with her, and frog-marched them off.

13 – An Unexpected Welcome

No sooner had the children turned out of sight than Jack's urgent whisper cut in from one side. *'Over 'ere! You gotta go! The moles just danced again!'* As they glanced to their right he stepped from behind a tree.

'Go *where?*' said Lucy, clearly put out.

'Home,' said Stella. She smiled apologetically.

'And where exactly *is* home?' said Lucy, frowning, '- and don't you *dare* to tell me it's in Australia!'

The children all laughed.

'It's not far,' said Stella brightly. 'Emma will tell you in the morning. I'm sorry. We will see you again, though!'

Lucy sniffed deeply, failing to hide her disappointment.

'Oh – and just in case…' Stella's cheeks reddened. She slipped the friendship bracelet off her wrist. 'Can you give this to Emma from me?'

'What on *earth's* that?' said Lucy with a frown, as Stella quickly slipped it onto her wrist.

'It's a friendship bracelet.' Stella smiled and shrugged her shoulders. 'It means you stay friends wherever you are!' Already the others were heading off. 'Thanks again, Lucy. You were brilliant! Emma will explain.' Then she turned and hurried towards the woods.

Jack insisted on rowing them back, even though he flinched each time his back brushed the edge of the boat. 'So much fer our midnight feast,' he chuckled. 'Got more than we bargained for there, eh?' Tom immediately started giggling.

Between them the children pulled the boat up under the tree.

'Well,' said Jack, suddenly awkward. 'I got you ter thank fer savin' me – an' fer savin' me pa by the sound o' things!' He cleared his throat. 'Was sure fine ter meet yer, an' 'ave a safe trip back!'

Stella swallowed hard. 'I hope your father gets well again quickly,' she said smiling.

'I'm sure 'e will now Mr Gladstone knows the truth. He'll be back at work in no time is my bet! An' fer the Gladstones most likely!

'Goodbye, littlun.' Jack held a grubby hand out to Tom. 'Yer's got spunk an' yer'll do well in life, nipper.' Tom smiled and nodded, clutching his trowel in one hand as Jack shook the other. 'An' you keep diggin'. Never know what's you might find in that garden o' yours!'

'I definitely will!' said Tom. 'Bye for now, Jack!' He climbed up onto the first tree nodule.

'Here, Jack, take this!' Stella held out the little orange torch. Tom's already done the tunnel in the dark - I'll just follow him!'

'Jeepers! Yer really meant it! Cheers!' With a delighted smile, Jack took the little torch and shone it up into the dark mass of branches. Stella grabbed onto the first nodule and was soon climbing up after Tom.

'Good luck!' Jack called after her. 'An' goodbye again!'

With the help of the torch beam Stella and Tom made quick progress and soon found themselves amongst the densely packed branches which, being so close together, were easy to locate once the torch light had faded.

'We're here!' whispered Tom, suddenly feeling earthen walls instead of tree trunk as he groped for the next branch. He quickly located the first ladder rung, stepped up onto the next branch up and found his head inside the tunnel.

'Time to go home,' he whispered as he peered up to a tiny well of daylight in the distance. 'See you again one day I hope, Jack.'

'Get a move on, will you!' urged his sister.

As the children crawled through the undergrowth for a second time, squinting at the daylight, a dry twig cracked outside the bush.

Tom and Stella froze on all fours, hardly daring to breathe. This time it really was Charlie Green's breathless snort. Moments later his green wellingtons appeared less than a metre from Tom's nose. 'What if he sees it?' each thought, two pairs of eyes fixed beyond the boots to the log on top of the mound.

'Come on out you two! I know you're in there!'

Tom and Stella crawled sheepishly out and were surprised to find Charlie Green now sitting on their log.

'Well,' he snorted, 'it ain't a bad idea. An' certainly not one worth hidin' in me bushes for.'

The children stood up brushing dirt and twigs from their hands, hair and knees.

'In fact,' continued, Charlie Green, 'it's a very good place for a seat. Nice spotta sunlight 'ere most mornings!' Tom and Stella reddened and smiled stiffly as Charlie Green handed them their lunch boxes. They then skipped off around the bush and out onto the lawn.

'What's got into him?' said Stella as she hurried along shoving sandwiches into her mouth.

Tom, disinterested in his food, was frowning.

'Back already,' murmured their father from behind his newspaper.

'Already? It's five o'clock, dear!' Their mother had paused from her piano playing as the children appeared.

'We met two sisters. They invited us in!' said Stella quickening her step across the room.

Their mother smiled. 'You see, dear! I *told* you it was only a matter of time!' She resumed her playing as Stella raced up the stairs chuckling.

As Tom entered his room he stopped and stared all

around. He tried to picture the enormous dining table, the red velvet chairs, the chandelier, and the enormous paintings. He then studied the wall separating his room from Stella's. Finally he turned to the fireplace.

'Stella! The initials!' They dived towards the fireplace and stuck their heads underneath. Tom's heart sank. Of course - the chimney was bricked up. He should have remembered. With his head hung low he stepped back onto his Earth Treasure Box, scattering its contents across the carpet.

'Cheer up, Tom!' said Stella brightly. 'We'll be able to go again sometime!' She opened Tom's French door window and stepped onto his tiny balcony. And now as she breathed in the sweet scent of orange blossom and looked out towards the trees she began to smile. 'Things here are definitely improving!' she would tell Hannah on Facebook that evening. She frowned thoughtfully. But how on earth would she code a message to say she'd travelled back in time across an underground lake?

Tom, in a world of his own, lay down on his bed. Something was bothering him. It wasn't the chimney, though he'd have liked to unblock it, there was something else. But he couldn't quite put his finger on it.

14 - The Forgotten Clue

Each day for the next week the children rose early to look for the moles, but they didn't appear. Stella passed the time composing coded Facebook messages to Hannah, and lazing with her music and piles of books in the patches of dappled sunlight on the lawn. Finally, she felt at peace in her new surroundings. She also felt sure that she would meet Emma again soon.

Tom, by contrast, grew quickly impatient. If he couldn't see his 'T' inside his chimney, then he wanted to bring back some other secret clue - some proof that their adventure had really happened. His mood wasn't improved when he started having nightmares about being back in the house with Stella, Emma and Jack. Each time without fail Crawley caught them from behind and locked them in a dark broom cupboard. And it was always at the point when the door swung back to reveal him stroking a long black whip that Tom woke drenched in sweat and shivering.

Charlie Green was usually hovering about in the

dream somewhere too, watching everything from a strange distance.

About ten days after their return from the time tunnel Tom awoke from just such a dream and lay looking around his room and listening to the birds singing outside. Finally he got out of bed and crossed to his window. He gazed across the sun-drenched lawn and began to wonder. Had he and Stella somehow *imagined* the whole adventure between them? Had their move from Hong Kong affected them in some strange way? Deep in thought he dressed himself. He crossed once more to the chimney. Once more he looked up inside at the solid bricks. Slowly he stood up and sighed. But then, as he turned and found himself staring at the three large stones that he had dug up at the beginning of the summer, and that now sat lined up at the foot of his bed, a sudden thought struck him - a thought as unexpected as lightning from a clear blue sky.

'Stella!' he shouted bursting into her room.

'What?' she said with a scowl. Hannah had left a message saying she thought joining a history club and taking up potholing were the most boring things she could imagine and, by the way, could Stella *please* write normally!

'Follow me!' said Tom holding up his trowel. 'I think I've found my proof from the past!'

'*Proof*?' But Tom had already shot out of the door. With a shake of her head Stella closed her Facebook page, then thundered down the stairs after him.

'*Tom what are you talking about?*' But her brother, who was tearing full pelt across the lawn, was too breathless to answer.

'It's somewhere around here!' he shouted, digging at a flowerbed in full view of the houses.

'Tom! You know you'll be grounded if Charlie Green catches you digging again!'

'I don't care! I *don't* care!' shouted Tom, now on hands and knees, flicking up earth in all directions, like a desperate animal. And then, quite suddenly, it appeared, almost exactly where he had thought it would. With the broadest of smiles Tom leaned down and with his thumb and forefinger pulled a small battered cloth purse from the soil - the purse he had dug up at the start of the summer and then discarded.

'What's *that*?' said Stella.

'Look!' he said proudly. 'It's *hers*. It's Mrs Gladstone's coin purse. The one they said was stolen. I thought it was a doll's purse when I dug it up last time.' He laid the purse flat in the palm of his hand. 'See - there!'

Stella screwed her eyes up and looked closely at the worn away cloth. Barely visible were two initials. The first she couldn't make out, but the second, if you looked carefully, resembled a very elaborate letter 'G'.

'G' for Gladstone,' whispered Tom. 'Crawley must have thrown it away in the garden and taken the money!'

'You been diggin' up them mole hills again?'

79

The air filled with an eerie silence. Tom and Stella momentarily froze before turning to meet the dark stare of Charlie Green. Immediately his eyes fell on the purse still lying in the palm of Tom's hand. For a split second Stella thought his gaze flickered. But then he shifted his stare back to Tom.

'Now, this really is your *last* warning, young Tom. Any more diggin' in this garden, I'll have yer grounded.' And with an expressionless gaze he stomped off.

'Why's that man *always* got it in for me?' said Tom crossly.

Stella stood curling a lock of her blonde hair around her finger and staring after Charlie. Then she gasped.

'Tom! Do you think *Charlie Green* knows about the time tunnel too?' Tom's eyes jumped wide.

'Maybe he takes Harry when he goes down it,' Stella went on. 'No wonder poor Mrs Moon's dotty!'

Tom stared into the distance thinking through his encounters with Charlie. Pieces of a complicated jigsaw seemed suddenly to be dropping into place.

'You know, there's one way we could find out more,' said Stella brightly.

'How's that?' murmured Tom, trying to gather his thoughts.

'Mrs Moon, of course! Charlie's always having cups of tea with her. I think we should pay her a visit!'

15 - Afternoon Tea

The following afternoon, Tom and Stella knocked on Mrs Moon's patio garden door.

'Good morning, Tom and Stella! How nice to see you, dears!' With the help of her walking stick Mrs Moon stepped out into her patio garden. It was strange how alert she could seem on some days compared with others. Their mother had told them she had an illness that made her forget things and people some of the time but not others. They were glad to have caught her on a good day.

'We called to see if Harry's back yet,' said Stella politely. Tom nodded enthusiastically. Harry had gone missing earlier that day.

'He's a one, isn't he!' exclaimed Mrs Moon. 'Went off this morning. But he'll be back by tonight, mark my words!' She winked playfully. 'He knows it's lamb you see!' Stella and Tom smiled. Mrs Moon chuckled. 'You know, the Williamsons next door are convinced he's got two homes! They're probably right!'

'Is Charlie working today?' Tom said suddenly.

Mrs Moon's gaze fell to the ground as she slowly picked her way across her patio towards a wrought iron chair in the shade of a small fig tree.

'Do sit down, dears,' she said, signalling with her stick towards a wooden bench. 'My legs aren't as strong as they used to be. Now, where were we? Oh, yes, Charlie. No, dears. He's not here on Fridays. Have you lost something in the garden, dears?'

'Oh no!' said Tom, reddening.

'Where does Charlie live, Mrs Moon?' asked Stella carefully.

'Up towards Kilburn, dear. About two miles from here.' She seemed to hesitate. 'He's a bit sharp with you little ones sometimes, I know. But he means well enough. He lives for the garden.' She took in a deep breath and looked out towards the trees.

'Where does Charlie think Harry goes?' asked Stella, popping a blackcurrant polo into her mouth and following Mrs Moon's gaze.

Mrs Moon smiled stiffly and shook her head. And now Stella regretted her remark for the old lady's eyes were suddenly glistening.

'Would you like some biscuits dears?'

Tom, ever hungry, nodded eagerly.

With the help of her stick Mrs Moon raised herself from her seat again.

'Can I help?' asked Stella, jumping up.

'No, no, dear.' The old lady tutted and shook her head, suddenly exasperated at her own frailty. 'You wait here, dears. I'll be back presently.' The children watched in silence as Mrs Moon slowly walked back across the patio leaning on her stick. She seemed to be muttering something to herself.

For a good five minutes that they sat politely waiting for the old lady to come back. In fact, they were just starting to think they'd been forgotten when she appeared in the doorway.

'My, oh my, visitors! How nice to see you, dears!' An awkward silence filled the air as Mrs Moon stepped forward and fixed a vacant stare on the children. Stella froze inside. Mrs Moon was looking at them most oddly. Suddenly Tom's tummy let out the most almighty rumble. Stella cleared her throat reprimandingly just as Mrs Moon jerked out of her trance.

'Dear me,' said the old lady, 'did I just go in for something? I could have sworn–'

'Biscuits!' said Tom sternly. He was starving, never mind bursting for a cold drink. Stella nudged him hard in the ribs, which made him yelp.

'Would you like a biscuit, dear? Oh, yes, that would be nice. Have you just moved to the garden? I don't suppose you've seen my dog have you? He's called Harry. He goes missing you know. For days at a time sometimes.' Tears were suddenly welling in the old lady's eyes.

Stella stood up. 'No, Mrs Moon, we haven't seen Harry,' she said gently. She took Mrs Moon by the arm and helped her sit down. 'But I'm sure he'll be back tonight. It's lamb for dinner you know!'

'My, oh my, is it Friday today?' said Mrs Moon. Stella nodded. 'What a clever girl you are! Well, it was nice to meet you, dear. I always like to see new faces in the garden. I think I shall have a lie down soon. I get so tired these days. Off you go and play now and come again tomorrow will you? I'll be less tired then. Goodbye then, dears!' The old lady was still nodding and smiling as the children walked away.

'Oh, well, that was a waste of time!' said Stella as they passed out of the gate.

'She's so sweet,' said Tom. '*How* could Charlie Green be so mean taking Harry from her?'

'We don't *know* that he does, Tom' said Stella. 'It was only an idea.'

Tom halted in his tracks and gave a deep frown. But as a dog's yelp echoed across the garden, the threads of his thoughts evaporated.

'*Look!* Here's Harry!' shrieked Stella. Harry was racing across the lawn towards them. As he shot in between them, droplets of cold water sprinkled their shins.

'Harry!' yelled Tom. But Harry didn't stop. Mrs Moon had been right about the lamb.

It took Tom and Stella about two seconds to have the same thought. Immediately they raced towards The Island and scrambled as fast as they could inside the rhododendron bush. But they were to be disappointed. The tunnel was nowhere to be found.

~

The following morning Charlie Green telephoned to say Mrs Moon had taken a bad turn and that he'd called a doctor and would their mother be able to sit with her for an hour later on.

Alarm bells immediately set ringing in Tom's head. This was a ploy. Charlie must have found out they'd been asking about him and didn't want them talking to the old lady again. But why?

'Charlie Green's onto us, Stell,' he said as soon as their mother had left the room. 'He's trying to keep us away so we don't tell Mrs Moon about Harry and the time tunnel! I think we should go there - right now! He might even have drugged her!'

Stella picked at her painted blue fingernails, deep in thought. 'Oh, I don't know, Tom. She is an old lady, and she is ill. You've seen how she gets!'

Later that day their mother returned from Mrs Moon's to confirm that the old lady was in bed and resting and would have 24-hour nurse care for the next few days.

'Seems she hasn't been eating enough! And that's very important at her ripe old age!'

'How old is she, then?' said Tom.

'She told me she was 105 on the day we moved in,' his mother replied with a chuckle. 'But I think that was on one of her confused days! Mind you, she can't be far off 100. And that's nearly as old as these houses!'

Tom stared through his mother and tried hard to imagine living for one hundred years, but the thought alone exhausted him. No wonder the old lady was in bed!

It was a full week later before Mrs Moon was finally well enough to receive visitors. Needless to say, Tom and Stella were both elated when the she rang to invite them back.

16 - The Return Visit

The first day of September had brought with it grey skies and an unseasonably sharp breeze, and the children stood shivering at Mrs Moon's back door. The patio garden was a far cry from the courtyard of dappled sunlight they had sat in a week earlier.

As she opened the door Mrs Moon's face lit up. 'Tom and Stella! How nice to see you, dears! Come along in, now, it's really quite blustery out there!'

Tom and Stella stepped quickly into Mrs Moon's kitchen. The old lady had renewed vigour, and a quickness of step they had never witnessed in her before. She immediately directed them through the hallway into a sitting room next door which was crammed full of dark furniture, covered here and there in lace cloths. A handsome standard lamp in one corner bathed the room in warm yellow light while a sombre looking man in an enormous portrait hanging above the fireplace eyed the children suspiciously.

The old lady followed their gaze upwards as she stood

leaning on her stick. 'Oh, don't worry about him, dears!' she chuckled. 'That's just Edward!' Tom and Stella each chose a chair and sat down.

'Who's Edward?' said Stella, adjusting the velvet cushion behind her.

Mrs Moon sat carefully down on an upright chair opposite the fireplace. 'That's better,' she said. 'You see, I know I can *get out* of this one! Ah, yes, Edward Moon, dear. My late husband. Such a lovely man.' She chuckled again to herself. 'You know we used to joke about that picture. We always said the young artist must have caught Edward on a bad day!' She paused for thought, then raised her small wrinkled hand to her mouth. 'Or was it the other way round? Dear me, I do seem to have forgotten!'

'It's beautifully painted,' said Stella, trying to sound like her mother.

'Well, yes, of course, dear. Anyway, enough of Edward. How *nice* it is to see you at last - and especially after my silly upset last week!'

'What upset?' said Tom, suspiciously.

Stella raised her eyes to the ceiling.

Mrs Moon smiled. 'Well, you know, dear, I wasn't quite myself at all. All that confusion. Anyway, Doctor Brown seems to have fixed me, and Charlie was brilliant as usual.'

Tom narrowed his eyes.

'I feel so much better,' Mrs Moon went on. 'Such

marvellous medicine they have these days. Would you like some juice dears? Apple or orange?'

'Orange please!' said Tom as the old lady slowly rose from her seat.

'Yes please,' said Stella. After their last visit she didn't like to offer to help, so instead she cast her eyes around in wonderment at the beautiful pictures and objects that crammed Mrs Moon's living room.

As the old lady disappeared back towards the kitchen Tom raised his eyebrows mischievously. Then, to Stella's alarm, he jumped up from his seat and started wandering from table to table fingering the array of silver-framed photographs, trinkets and ornaments that filled almost every surface. This was the stuff of his dreams - a real, live treasure trove!

'Leave them alone!' whispered Stella crossly.

She could hear Mrs Moon pottering about in the kitchen next door. But Tom, being Tom, ignored her, and when he had completed a circuit of the room he delivered his sister a cheeky grin then disappeared through another doorway.

Stella jumped up from her seat to give chase just as Mrs Moon reappeared pushing a large trolley. On the top shelf sat a silver teapot, blue floral milk jug, teacup and saucer, and two glasses of orange juice. On the lower shelf sat a large silver platter crammed with an assortment of biscuits.

'Tom!' Stella called crossly, her eyes glued to the

biscuits. Then she remembered herself. 'I'm sorry about my brother,' she said, then smiled politely at Mrs Moon. 'He's rather nosy I'm afraid.' Tom appeared at the other doorway looking strangely embarrassed.

'I see you've found my bedroom, Tom!' said Mrs Moon taking up the biscuit plate. 'Did you find anything interesting, dear?' She winked playfully at him. Tom smiled awkwardly and sat down. His normally rosy cheeks had drained and as Stella selected a pink iced biscuit she couldn't help but smirk that her brother for once had been caught out.

'Would you like a biscuit, dear?'

'No thanks,' Tom said weakly.

Stella almost choked on her orange juice. She had never known *Tom* refuse a biscuit!

Everyone paused for thought. Then Tom spoke again.

'Where's Harry, Mrs Moon? And Charlie Green?' He was in defiant mood and obviously didn't give two hoots about giving the old lady a heart attack.

Stella cleared her throat impatiently, then held her breath in anticipation.

'Ah, yes, dear, Harry!'

Mrs Moon leaned forward from her chair with a strange smile, then, with a shaking arm, poured herself a cup of tea. She sat back, took a sip from her cup then lowered it decisively onto the saucer. As the clank of china reverberated around the room Stella and Tom both flinched. Now, as the old lady cleared her throat, Stella knew that she was about to make her announcement.

Stella crunched hard on her biscuit and stared beyond Mrs Moon trying not to look too interested. As she did so, she fixed her gaze on an old trunk covered in a white lace cloth, down to the side of Mrs Moon's chair. As the old lady began to speak Stella's stare remained fixed on this seemingly obscure piece of furniture, and yet the longer she stared the faster her heart began to beat.

Mrs Moon started to say something about Harry and Charlie but suddenly Stella wasn't listening. By now her cheeks were burning. Her eyesight wasn't bad, but in the dim yellow light she couldn't be sure of what she was seeing.

With her head spinning, Stella downed her glass of orange juice in one and plonked it on the trolley in front of her.

'Is there any more juice?' she blurted out.

An awkward silence filled the room as Stella felt her cheeks turn purple. She then gave Mrs Moon the most enormous grin. This rudeness wasn't like her at all, but she just *had* to get a look at that trunk.

With a look of surprise Mrs Moon began to raise herself from the chair. 'Why, of course there is, dear. Help me up will you, Tom.'

'Shall I get it?' Tom offered politely.

Stella looked at her brother in astonishment. First refusing biscuits. Now offering to *help* someone! Exactly what had come over him in the last five minutes?

'No, no, dear. I'm fine,' said Mrs Moon gently. 'You sit down. I shall be right back.'

'*Hey, Stella*!' Tom could barely contain himself.

But Stella didn't hear him. She was already at the side of the trunk.

'Look, Tom! *Look!*' she whispered excitedly.

Though worn in places, the gold lettering was clear enough. And yet, as she took the deepest of breaths, Stella could barely believe what she was reading. But there it was - clear as daylight: *Miss S E Gladstone*.

Tom was quickly at his sister's side, and as he crouched down and read the words a broad grin spread out across his face.

'*Sophie Gladstone!*' Stella gasped in a whisper. 'Mrs Moon must be *Sophie!*'

17 - Unmasked

'Dear, me, I see you've beaten me to my story, dears!'
The children jumped up in alarm. Mrs Moon stood in the
doorway holding Stella's glass of orange juice. She had a
strange smile on her face as she fixed a vacant stare on
the children. And now Stella remembered. This was the
stare she had given them that day in the patio garden. It
was a stare that at the time had felt familiar, but which
she had cast aside in her mind.

'Sophie Gladstone?' said Stella in astonishment. 'Is
your real name *Sophie Gladstone*?'

Mrs Moon's face lit up with amusement. 'Oh, dear me,
no!' she chuckled. 'No, dears! *Look!*' Her face was
beaming as she gestured with her stick towards a second
trunk sitting in the far corner by the window. 'There's
mine, over there, dears!'

Stella walked slowly across the room towards the
trunk, her heart thumping against her chest. As she
crouched down and carefully lifted the white lace a haze
of tears blurred her vision. But it didn't matter of course.

She knew what the letters would say. After a moment's pause she wiped her eyes, then with quivering voice she read the name out loud: 'Miss E M Gladstone'.

Mrs Moon placed the glass of orange juice on the trolley. 'That's right, dears,' she said gently. '*I* am Emma Gladstone, the same young Emma you met when you travelled down the time tunnel.' She shook her head and sighed deeply as her eyes started to glisten. 'Dear me, it all seems *such* a long time ago!'

Stella stood up and stared across at the old lady, already searching for signs of Emma.

Suddenly the old lady smiled at Tom. Then she winked. 'Tom had guessed, hadn't you, dear?' To Stella's surprise, Tom gave a triumphant grin. She turned towards her brother in disbelief.

'But how, Tom? How could you possibly have known?'

Mrs Moon nodded towards the door Tom had disappeared through earlier. 'Tom the unstoppable!' she said chuckling. 'I should have known you'd go snooping in there, Tom! Go along now, dear. Show your big sister.'

As Stella followed Tom into the bedroom her eyes froze open. The walls were crammed with large gilt-framed portraits, each one bearing the name 'Gladstone' on a bronze coloured plaque at the bottom. But Tom ignored these paintings. Instead, under the solemn gaze of the various members of the Gladstone family, he strode around the bed and to the far end of the room. There, in pride of place above a fireplace, hung by far the smallest picture.

As she approached, Stella saw it was of a young dark-haired girl holding a small dog. *'E. M. Gladstone'* read the tag across the bottom. It was the same picture they had seen in the Gladstones' dining room when they travelled down the time tunnel.

'Emma Margaret Gladstone,' said Mrs Moon from the doorway. 'And Harry, of course. Dearest Harry! But come now. Let's sit down again. There really is so much to tell.'

Stella's mind buzzed with questions as they left the bedroom. Could this old lady *really* be Emma? Was it possible she was still alive after all that time? If this was her, what was she doing living in a different house in the garden? And what did Charlie Green have to do with all this?

The children sat down again. 'Well, dears,' said Mrs Moon slowly, 'I do believe I owe you an explanation.' She smiled as she looked each of them in the eye. 'No doubt you've both been wondering if your adventure wasn't just a silly dream!'

The children nodded in silence.

'Well, my dears, I can tell you now it *wasn't* a dream.' She shook her head and chuckled. 'I shall never forget the day Harry found you behind that bush when we were out having lessons with Miss Walker! And do you remember the look on my face, Tom, when Jack dropped down the chimney breast!' Tom could only smile and nod as his throat went tight.

'You know, I was sure it was going to be my good friend Lucy,' said Mrs Moon, 'all ready to look for the moles. What a shock it all was! But, oh, *what* an adventure!'

And now as the old lady's eyes began to sparkle, Stella could see. How delicately time had traced itself into her small pale face. Yet, despite the wrinkles, she was still very beautiful. The child's face was still in there. The dark round eyes, eager for adventure. This was Emma all right. Her youthful spirit had never left her, it had simply got buried as she had grown older.

'I'm sorry we had to leave you,' said Stella weakly. 'We really wanted to bring you with us, you know.'

'Oh, don't you go worrying yourself about that, dear,' said Mrs Moon brightly. 'My adventure didn't end there you know!' Tom and Stella sat up in surprise as the old lady gave a mischievous grin.

'You see, my dears, two days later Lucy and I went on our mole hunt after all! I'd told her about you two and the time tunnel of course. She was desperate to come and meet you again. It was her idea that we should look for the tunnel as soon as possible.'

Now the old lady's eyes sparkled again. 'And do you know what, Tom and Stella?' She clutched her chest like an excited young child. 'The moles danced for us - and we rowed across the lake and *found the tunnel!*'

Tom was leaning so far forward he almost fell off his chair.

'Where did it take you?' asked Stella. She held her breath, hardly daring to think what she might hear next.

'Well,' said Mrs Moon, sitting back, 'I was hoping we would be able to visit you in the same time as you had come from, but instead we came out in the garden at a time *beyond even today!*'

Stella put her hand to her mouth just as Tom's chair collapsed on the floor behind him.

'Wow! Did you see *aliens* and stuff?' he cried scrambling up.

Stella shot him an impatient glance as Mrs Moon smiled and gazed towards the window. 'You know, dears, the garden was still as enchanting and happy a place as ever, filled with children's laughter and fun.' She breathed in deeply and sat looking at the children.

'Mrs Moon...what *did* you find?' asked Stella nervously.

The old lady hesitated. Then she smiled. 'Well, all I will say, Stella, is I am sure you will both enjoy the garden for *many* years to come!'

Stella bit her bottom lip as she tried to take in what Mrs Moon had just said. Did this mean they were going to meet Emma again in the *future*? Somehow she knew that she couldn't ask.

'But you did go back home afterwards, didn't you?' she said.

'Oh yes, of course we did, dear. But we got into a lot

of trouble, you know.'

Tom and Stella leaned forward, eager to hear more.

'You see we had stayed away for three days! The police were called and they went on at us so much in the end we told our story. Of course no-one believed us, and we couldn't prove it. My father never really forgave me for making him look so foolish. It was all over the newspapers.'

A wave of sadness broke across Mrs Moon's face, but passed as quickly as it had appeared. 'By the time I left home and met Edward I'd started using my middle name, Margaret.'

'But why?' said Stella.

'Well, you know, everyone I met as I was growing up seemed to remember the Emma Gladstone time tunnel story and it all got so tiresome in the end.'

The old lady stared up at the portrait again. 'Edward died twenty years ago. We hadn't any children, and it was only then I decided to move back to the garden. With the houses all divided into flats now it's perfect for me. I do so love it here.'

'But what about Harry?' said Stella suddenly.

Mrs Moon chuckled. 'Of course! Dearest Harry! That's who we were talking about when this all started! Well, Harry was given to me as a puppy for my fifth birthday. We lived for each other. My mother had that picture painted of us just after I got him. I missed him terribly when he finally died.'

To the children's surprise, a child like grin now spread across the old lady's face. 'But then, you know what, Tom and Stella? It was a few days after I moved back here to the garden - Harry came back!'

'Came back?' they exclaimed.

'I could barely believe it myself,' said Mrs Moon chuckling. 'You see, I had got up early and gone for a walk in the garden. I've always woken early since Edward died. And then, out of the blue, there they were! The moles again!'

The old lady frowned and tutted. 'They vanished as quickly as they appeared, so naturally I thought I'd imagined it. But then, as I was walking back to my flat, he appeared - racing across the lawn. Soaking wet. It was Harry all right. I'd know my Harry anywhere!'

Confused thoughts flashed through Stella's mind as she tried to take in what she'd heard. 'Mrs Moon, are you telling us that *your* Harry here is the *same* Harry you had as a child?'

'That's right, dear!' said Mrs Moon beaming. 'And, you know, it all makes so much sense!' She gazed out towards the garden. 'Harry's coming and going didn't bother me at first. I knew he must have found a way to travel between me and my old time. Perhaps the moles divulge themselves to animals more readily? Who knows? *'He's gone to see the young me!'* I would chuckle to myself on the days I remembered things clearly.

'You see,' she went on, 'I believe Harry doesn't want

me to grow lonely in my old age and that's why he keeps coming to see me. It also explains his absences when I was a child.'

Now the old lady looked down.

'But then you know, dears, age has a way of playing tricks on you. I'm over 100 now, and my memory comes and goes from one day to the next. That means I don't always remember about Harry - or our adventure.'

'Wow!' said Tom, beaming with admiration.

The old lady continued. 'You know, I do wonder if the moles have something to do with my long life - and Harry's. He lived until he was 16, you know. That was quite a record back in those days!'

Stella stared in silent astonishment. Perhaps what Mrs Moon had told their mother about her age hadn't been so wrong after all.

Mrs Moon paused, then gave the children a strange smile. 'You know, Tom and Stella, I feel happy now. I think Harry may have returned to the young Emma for good - to live his life out in peace. That's why I wanted to talk to you. Before it gets too late.'

Stella tried hard to swallow, but a lump had risen in her throat. Was Mrs Moon telling them she was about to die?

The old lady leaned forward and pointed with her frail hand towards a side table. 'Look, Stella, in there.'

Slowly Stella raised herself from her chair and pulled open the mahogany drawer. Her friendship bracelet, its cotton threads now worn and faded, lay on top of a pile of folded white napkins. She bowed her head, trying to hide her tears as she remembered Hannah's words.

'I think you should take it, dear,' said Mrs Moon with a gentle smile.

Tom suddenly jumped up. 'Mrs Moon,' he blurted out, 'what's Charlie Green got to do with all this? Has he been down the time tunnel too?'

Stella shot him an impatient glance.

Mrs Moon sat back in surprise.

'Bless me, no dear!' the old lady chuckled. Then she paused and cleared her throat. 'But, oh, I think I *do* see why you're asking.' She studied the carpet for a few moments then raised her eyes towards Tom.

'Well, Tom, I have to confess that Charlie does know about the time tunnel. And that you went down it – in fact he knew about that before you did!'

Tom and Stella exchanged looks of disbelief.

'You see, dears, what with Harry's coming and going all soaking wet I felt I really had to explain, in case he stopped him going back. Anyway, he was wonderful about it.' She shook her head and smiled. 'You know, I think it was only when you two moved here that he really believed me! He's always been very protective about the molehills since I told him, and I'm sorry, Tom, if he's been a bit sharp about them.'

'But why didn't you tell us you were Emma?' asked Tom.

The old lady smiled. 'How could I, dear? You needed to go and rescue Jack. I didn't dare interfere with that. And then what with my memory–'

A grandfather clock chimed in the shadows.

'Dear me, is that the time?' said Mrs Moon in a fluster. 'Nurse Goodson will be here presently. You really must be getting home, dears.'

They all stood up and slowly she led them out to the kitchen.

'Well, children, it was wonderful to see you again!' she said. 'And I'm so glad I've been able to share my story with you at last.'

'We'll come and see you tomorrow,' said Stella brightly. 'There's only one more week of the holidays left.' Tom nodded in solemn agreement as they stepped out into cold.

'Of course, dears. Goodbye, dears!' And Mrs Moon closed the door.

18 - Journey's End

The next morning before breakfast Tom and Stella's mother called them into the sitting room and gently broke the news that Mrs Moon had died peacefully during the night.

The children stared at the wall behind their mother, each trying to take in what they had heard. Tears of frustration immediately began welling in Tom's eyes. Why oh why did Mrs Moon have to go and die now? Just when their adventure had begun again? There was still so much to talk about. So much to try to understand. And with Mrs Moon's help he felt certain they could have found the time tunnel and gone back again.

Stella, sitting quietly beside him, was trying to imagine what dying or being dead must feel like. She felt strangely calm on hearing the news; content that Mrs Moon was at last at peace with her beloved Harry. At the same time it occurred to her that by going back down the time tunnel they could, she supposed, if they got the dates right, bring Mrs Moon back to life again and carry on with their secret adventure. Then she thought about what Mrs Moon had told them. Perhaps they would meet her again one day in the future? After all, she had hinted at this, hadn't she?

But then, without warning, it hit her. Mrs Moon, Emma, was gone. They would probably *never* see her again. 'What about Harry?' she whispered, as one after the other the tears rolled down her cheeks.

Her mother sat down and put her arms around her.

'Not a sign of him anywhere. He hasn't been seen for over a week now. You know what? *I* think Margaret's gone to find him!'

Stella tugged at a lock of her long blonde hair and began gently sobbing as she mulled over a host of unspeakable thoughts.

~

'I feel sorry for Charlie,' said Stella on the morning after the funeral as they sat watching him pottering around by his shed in the distance. 'He looks so *lonely* all of a sudden. Look how much more slowly he's moving about. He seems to have his head bowed down all the time.'

Tom frowned at the grass between his shoes. He felt let down by Charlie Green - angry at him for not letting on he knew.

'He's coming this way!' whispered Stella suddenly. She scrambled to her feet, slowly followed by Tom.

Charlie was walking towards them carrying a hold-all, and as he approached they could see dark circles around his eyes, as if he hadn't slept for a week.

Tom, who felt his cheeks turn purple, stared at the ground. Stella swallowed hard. As Charlie now stood before them she wanted to say something, but she didn't know how.

'She was a wonderful lady was Margaret,' he said, gently, 'an' you know that better than most, don't you?' He gave them a warm smile then looked across towards The Island. 'Still, she's happy now, with Harry an' all.'

'I know,' said Stella. Her arms hung heavily at her side.

Charlie stepped forward and bowed his head towards Tom. 'I never meant to be gruff, Tom. It was just the moles. I was worried about them moles. You know how important they were to her – and Harry.'

Tom smiled stiffly, trying hard to avoid his stare. But then, as Charlie put his hand gently on his shoulder, a wave of warmth surged through him, sweeping away all of his anger. With relief, he found himself looking up at Charlie and smiling. And despite everything, it felt like the most natural thing in the world.

'Well, it's getting late,' said Charlie picking up his hold-all. 'Time for me to head off.' He smiled and gave a friendly wink. 'An' don't you go worryin' about your secret now. It's safe as houses with me!' He slowly turned and plodded off.

Tom and Stella sat back down and watched Charlie disappear around the corner, Stella all the while smiling to herself as she lightly twirled her friendship bracelet. Already she had bought new threads and would begin renewing it before they started school.

Tom lay back down on the grass and peered at the sky through the great arms of the tree. How relieved he felt to be free at last from the anger and suspicion he had felt about Charlie ever since they had moved to the garden.

Half an hour later they headed in for lunch. 'Charlie was here a while ago,' said their mother as she dished pasta into three bowls. He left something for you both on the table there.' She smiled and winked. 'Said it was top secret and that you should open it in private!'

Tom immediately lunged at the small brown packet that lay on the kitchen table, then dashed outside. Stella followed right behind. Tom tore at the paper, then – thump! – out fell Stella's orange torch, battered and worn, onto the patio table. Stella clapped her hand to her mouth. Tom stood staring in silence, his heart starting to race.

'There's a note!' squealed Stella.

Tom snatched up the piece of paper. As he opened it out, the creases made a perfect cross where it had been folded into four. And now, as they read what was written in front of them, neither Tom nor Stella flinched.

Dear Tom and Stella

I meant to return this torch you gave my father sooner, but what with Mrs Moon falling ill I'm afraid I forgot.

My father told me all about how he came by it – quite a story that was! 'Flash Jack and his light,' people used to call him - he got up to all sorts of tricks with it!

You know he worked here when I was a boy – just like my grandfather did before him. That's how I got to know the gardens – and the magical moles!

I'm going to miss Margaret now she's gone. I would have told her more about my family when I realised she was Emma Gladstone, but I didn't want to add to her confusion. Still, I hope I helped her get along in her final years by helping Harry come and go through the tunnel.

Well, my time here's spent. There's gardens up near where I live need tending to. I'm not as young as I used to be and it'll be easier working closer to home.

I'm sorry we can't spend more time together. Still, I hope you'll continue to enjoy the garden! Look after each other, won't you – and mind them moles!

Charles Green

'Charlie's Jack's son!' gasped Tom.

He threw the note down and raced out through the patio gate into the gardens.

'Charlie! Where are you?' he yelled. 'Charlie! Charlie!' The name echoed all around the garden and up through the trees and seemed for a moment to become part of everything.

'What on earth's all that about?' said their mother staring out of the door.

Stella snatched up the letter and stuffed it into her jeans pocket. 'Just Tom gone a bit bonkers!' she said with a smile. She grabbed the torch from the patio table and dashed through the gate after him.

'He's gone, Stella, he's gone.' Tom fought to hold back the tears as he walked back towards her.

Stella stood and gazed out across the lawn towards The Island.

'Well,' she said with a smile, 'we were right after all about him using the tunnel, weren't we? How kind of him to help Margaret like that. It's exactly the sort of thing Jack would have done!'

Tom nodded as he followed Stella's gaze out across the lawn.

Stella took a deep breath in, then sighed. 'At least we now know for sure that we didn't dream all of this!'

With a huge smile, she put her arm around her brother's shoulders and squeezed him close.

As they walked back to the house, Tom felt surprisingly calm. He knew this was the end of their secret adventure - and yet in a strange sort of way it felt like a new beginning.

'Mum!' he said brightly as they stepped back through the kitchen door.

Stella squinted warily at him.

'When I'm older, mum, I'm going to buy this flat from you, *and* the one above, *and* the one above that. Actually,' he went on, his eyes widening with every word, 'it's going to be my home. With *real* fireplaces and everything. Just like in the olden days!'

His mother chuckled. 'Why, whatever made you think of that, Tom!'

Tom grinned across at Stella and slowly but surely drew the letter 'T' in the air.

Unseen by her mother Stella popped a lime-flavoured polo into her mouth and, as her ears began to tingle, she grinned across at her brother. Tom had made his mind up, and there would be no stopping him!

~

Please write a review

Authors love hearing from their readers!

Please let Karen Inglis know what you thought about
The Secret Lake by leaving a review on **thesecretlake.com**

Karen will always reply to you :)

If under age 13, please ask a grown-up to help you.

And if they can help you copy your review to Amazon or
your other preferred online bookstore it will help more
parents and children find *The Secret Lake*.

Top Tip: be sure not to give away any of the story's
secrets when writing your review!

Stay in touch...

Sign up to Karen's Readers' Club at
kareninglisauthor.com/TSLreadersclub for a free
poster of The Secret Lake's front cover, and a fun
crossword puzzle with clues based on the story.

You'll also be the first to hear about Karen's new books,
author events and special offers, including the chance to
become an advance reader for new titles.

If under age 13, please ask a grown-up to sign up for you.

About the author

kareninglisauthor.com

Karen Inglis lives in London, England. She has two sons, George and Nick, who inspired her to write when they were younger. Karen also writes for business, but has much more fun making up stories!

ALSO BY KAREN INGLIS

- Eeek! The Runaway Alien (7-10 yrs)
- Walter Brown and the Magician's Hat (7-10 yrs)
- Henry Haynes and the Great Escape (6-8 yrs)
- The Tell-Me Tree (4-8 years)
- Ferdinand Fox's Big Sleep (3-5 yrs)
- Ferdinand Fox and the Hedgehog (3-6 years)
- The Christmas Tree Wish (3-6 years)

Turn the page to find out more! >>>

facebook.com/kareninglisauthor

twitter.com/kareninglis

instagram.com/kareninglis_childrensbooks

ALSO BY KAREN INGLIS
IN PRINT AND AS EBOOKS

* Eeek! The Runaway Alien (7-10 yrs)

Eleven-year-old Charlie can't believe his luck when he opens his door to an alien one morning — a football-mad alien who's run away to Earth to be with him for the World Cup!

* Walter Brown and the Magician's Hat (7-9+ yrs)

When Walter Brown inherits a magician's hat from his Great Grandpa Horace on his 10th birthday he discovers it has special powers, and that his cat Sixpence is no ordinary cat. Magical mayhem follows…!

*Henry Haynes and the Great Escape (6-8 yrs)

After Henry complains that his library book is boring, he gets sucked down inside where he meets Brian, a bossy boa constrictor, and Gordon, a *very* smelly gorilla with a zoo escape plan. Brian and Gordon want Henry's help...!

* Ferdinand Fox's Big Sleep (3-5 yrs)

"Ferdinand Fox curled up in the sun,
as the church of St Mary struck quarter past one…"
A delightful colour picture book based on the true story of a fox that once fell asleep in the author's garden. Children love the rhyming text, counting as the clock strikes from one to five and discussing the food we see in Ferdinand's dream bubbles!

Ferdinand Fox and the Hedgehog (3-6 yrs)

"As soon as she smelled the scent of a fox,
she scampered to hide in an old soggy box."

Introducing Hatty the hedgehog and little Ed who meet
Ferdinand Fox when out hunting for bugs one night. Includes
eight pages of photos and fun facts about foxes and hedgehogs.

The Christmas Tree Wish (3-5+ yrs)

A heart-warming Christmas tale about hope, friendship and
being different. As the snow starts to fall on Christmas Eve
morning, little Bruce Spruce dreams about finding a home for
Christmas Day. But when things don't quite go to plan he finds
that his friends are there for him – and all is not lost...

The Tell-Me Tree (4-8 yrs)

Hello, I am the Tell-Me Tree. Why don't you come and sit by me…"
Beautifully illustrated, this gentle picture book invites children
to share how they are feeling – whether happy, sad or
somewhere in between – through conversation, drawing or
writing, with friends, family or trusted grown-ups .
Includes links to free activity sheets and other resources for use
at home or in the classroom.

**Order online, from your local bookshop or at
kareninglisauthor.com**